Jen,

One of

I love Karter & Jack. Jack's mom & Oscar make it rich.

Thanks for being you — you make the world richer.

Scott Hildreth

Karter

Scott Hildreth

This book is a work of fiction. Names, characters, places, and incidents are the product of the author's imagination or are used fictitiously. Any resemblances to actual events, locales, or persons living or dead, are coincidental.

Copyright © 2014 by Scott Hildreth

All rights reserved. In accordance with the U.S. Copyright Act of 1976, the scanning, uploading, and electronic sharing of any part of this book without the permission of the author or publisher constitute unlawful piracy and theft of the author's intellectual property. If you would like to use the material from the book (other than for review purposes), prior written permission must be obtained by contacting the author at designconceptswichita@gmail.com. Thank you for your support of the author's rights.

Published by
Eralde Publishing

Cover Design Copyright © Creative Book Concepts
Text Copyright © Scott Hildreth
Formatting by Creative Book Concepts

ISBN 13: 978-0692339640
All Rights Reserved

DEDICATION

This book is dedicated to any and all friends of Bill W.

PROLOGUE

"What in the fuck is this? Are you God damned kidding me? I told you to get wet and fucking sandy. Didn't I? That's a piss poor excuse for wet and sandy. You're going to fuck around and kill a teammate from your team, aren't you?" the instructor bellowed as he pointed at my wet and sparsely sand covered torso.

I closed my eyes, opened my mouth, and attempted to scream, "No sir."

The sound emitted from my mouth was scratchy and weak. I had completed the five mile run in an unsatisfactory time and was being punished for it. The human mind is simply incapable of comprehending the depth of the physical conditioning necessary to complete training to become a Navy SEAL. Regardless of a recruit's intent, devotion, desire or perceived state of readiness prior to arrival; to actually be physically, mentally or emotionally prepared would be impossible.

He pointed toward the ocean and began screaming a blood curdling howl, "Run back out to the US Navy's Pacific Ocean and dip yourself in it Jack-off. The Navy built this beach for me to drown you in, did you know that? I'm sick and motherfucking tired of screaming your name. Get wet Jack-off, and get sandy. Wet and fucking sandy. Lives depend on it."

The instructor's voice had become horse during our short duration of training. I was certain the sound of his strained vocal cords was solely due to my lack of ability. He had spent the majority of his time screaming

KARTER

at one person and one person only.

Me.

Exhausted, I ran as fast as I could and dove into the ocean face first. As I landed, sand and small sea shells filled my mouth. I closed my eyes to protect them from the salty water and waited for the next wave to wash over me. Now soaked from head to toe, I rose from the beach and ran the distance from the edge of the water to where he stood waiting. Satisfied I would be relieved of my punishment and sent to join the remainder of the class, I planted my boots firmly in the sand and attempted to stand erect. He stared at me as if I had committed a sinful act. His eyes resembled what I expected the devil's to look like. As his face began to quiver from what was undoubtedly a fit of anger, he opened his mouth and did his best to scream.

"You're not going to make it. You're a fucking idiot. Please do us both a favor and D.O.R, Jack-off. Drop out. Ring the fucking bell three times and go join the fucking Army. You'll never be a SEAL. I gave you simple fucking instructions, Jack-off. Wet and motherfucking sandy. You ran to my fucking ocean and washed your stupid self off, didn't you? You took a fucking bath in my God forsaken ocean. I gave you two tasks; two things, Jack-off. Wet and *what*? What was your mission?"

I stood and stared, confused.

Go get wet Jack-off and get sandy.

Shit.

Wet and *sandy*.

I had forgotten the *sandy* portion of his instructions. Five days into this phase of training and I would likely be killed by the instructor in a fit of rage. If not, only two and a half more years of punishing training and I would be deployed as a Navy SEAL. I parted my lips and moved my sandy tongue to the roof of my mouth, attempting to clear it of the debris from the beach.

"Wet and sandy," I responded in a gravelly tone.

He crossed his arms over his massive chest, "Are you fucking sandy, Jack-off?"

I lieu of responding, I dropped to the surface of the beach as if my legs had been cut from underneath me. Flat on my back, I frantically flipped my arms through the sand, doing my best to cover every respective inch of my wet torso with the small granules. Satisfied my entire body was completely covered; I scooped up a handful of sand and dumped it onto my wet face.

Silence.

He's not screaming, he must like what I'm doing.

I reached out and retrieved another handful of official US Navy sand. I opened my mouth and released it onto my face. As the sand filled my mouth and fell into my throat, his voice broke the silence.

"This is the first thing you only half fucked up today, Jack-off. In the time it took you to complete the task, I'm sure no less than three of your teammates would have been killed. You're only concerned with yourself. You're wet and sandy, but three men have died in the process. Outfuckingstanding. Get out of my face. Go away. I feel ill. Your incompetence and lack of desire is making me sick," he barked.

I jumped to my feet and attempted to run. As I brushed the sand from my eyes, I saw my class standing along the beach in the distance. Assembled into seven man boat crews and holding rubber rafts over their heads, their bodies shook from exhaustion. My tired legs quivered underneath me as I attempted to propel myself forward. As I stumbled toward my class in an unintended zig-zag pattern, my mind filled with wonder. Without a doubt, upon my arrival yet another instructor would start punishing me. In the eyes of the instructor and the US Navy, at least one of the teams would be one man short until I arrived. In my mind this class would *always* be one man short.

Graham and I had agreed to join the Navy together. We went to the barber and had our long locks of hair buzzed off as a team. We walked into the recruiter's office side-by-side, and after an assurance of being able to receive our training together, joined under the US Navy's buddy program. We were inseparable. We were invincible. We were best friends. Settling for nothing short of becoming Navy SEALs, we began training at home as we waited for the day we were scheduled to ship off.

Graham never made it to training. An accident a week before shipping out ended his life at seventeen years of age.

I closed my eyes and attempted to find a few ounces of inner strength. As my boots dug into the loose sand, I swung my arms and screamed. Now in an all-out run toward my class, I mentally prepared myself for what may be next.

The only easy day was yesterday.

KARTER

"Hi my name's Karter and I'm a drug addict."

"Hi Karter."

"I think I'll just listen."

"Thanks Karter," the group said in unison.

The thought of a group of people attempting to shove God down my throat and assuring me if I didn't *find* him, I couldn't make improvements to my life was a bit more than I was willing to try to listen to.

Or believe.

To me, God had always been a ghost. Something half the people *believed* in. The other half was split in two, the portion who *wondered*, and the portion who *didn't believe*.

And I didn't believe in ghosts.

"Karter, you need to share," she strung my name along until it was two five second long syllables separated by one overly long period of silence.

I slowly turned to my left and looked over my shoulder in disgust at the counselor who partially blocked the doorway into the meeting room. It was day one in what was to be a twenty-eight day drug rehab program, and I was attending my first twelve step meeting. My problem wasn't drugs. My only real issue, if there was one, was my mouth.

"Isn't it some form of invasion of privacy? You being here? I think

KARTER

you should be in your fucking office and let us advance through this program at our own pace. This meeting is for addicts, not assholes," I smirked slightly and blinked my eyes repeatedly.

"I *am* an addict Karter, just like you. Please share with the group. Anything. Say something, even if it's a small something," she pleaded softly as she crossed her arms in front of her chest.

The group remained silent as they waited for me to speak. The room smelled like the combination of a cafeteria in a shitty hospital and a wet can of coffee grounds. I rolled my eyes and turned around. I surveyed the numerous faces and eventually became focused on the wicker basket in the center of the table. I stared at the small pile of folded pieces of paper and considered what to say.

I looked around the room.

Sixteen, including me.

All I needed to do was complete the program, go in front of the judge and convince him I was a drug addict. If he believed me to be in the process of recovering, I would get my driver's license and my life back. Even I should be able to make it twenty-eight days.

"Hi my name's Karter and I'm a drug addict," I paused and raised my fingers to my mouth.

"Hi Karter."

As I nibbled what little black polish remained on my fingernails, I began to explain what happened to the best of my ability. I've never really had a problem talking to people, but I didn't care much for authority. The staff member standing in the doorway with her eyes fixed on the back of my head was grinding on my nerves.

"You know how there's always someone who seems more interested in your business than they should be? Some absolute asshole who is repeatedly peering over your shoulder? Maybe it's simply a figure of speech and they're not *really* behind you taking your inventory," I paused and glanced over my left shoulder.

"But they're watching you none the less, waiting for you to fuck up," I said as I turned and faced the group.

Heads bobbed up and down like they were on springs. Several people gave some form of slight verbal confirmation. I took a slow aggravated breath through my nose as I thought of my bike being in an impound yard, undoubtedly being rained on while I was attempting to entertain a group of fifteen has beens, fuck ups, and wards of the legal system.

"Well, those types of people seem to flock to me. One of them called the cops and I ended up in a psych ward for an evaluation. My only way out of the psych ward was to admit I was an addict. You know, give them a reason for me being there. So, that's what I did. The judge required I attend a treatment program. This one was twenty-eight days instead of thirty, and I thought I may make it twenty-eight, but I had my doubts about thirty," I grinned and raised my eyebrows as I looked down at my fingernails.

Silence.

"Glad you're here, Karter," someone said from across the table.

I looked up. He was staring at my tits.

"Stare much?" I asked as I pulled my hand from my mouth.

I'd like to dig your eyes out, you douchebag.

His gaze immediately shifted to the person beside me. I shook my head lightly and looked down at my nails. It seemed all men were the same. If a girl was anything remotely close to attractive, men didn't care who she was. Immediately, their minds shifted to thoughts of sex. I liked sex as much as any man if not more, but I generally wanted to know a little about who I was going to be fucking before we got started. Generally speaking, men gave me an ice cream headache. If I had my bike and a blank canvas, I didn't so much need a man.

I sat and admired my tattoos silently as several people spoke. When a man from across the table began to speak, either the beginning of the story or the tone of his voice captured my attention. Whichever it was, I looked up and listened intently as he began. The more he spoke, the more attentive I became.

"My name's Bill, and to me this program's simple. Breathe in, breathe out, and don't take a drink between breaths. As easy as it is, I seem to fuck up regularly. I'm seventy-two, and I've been in this program for forty years and in treatment half a dozen or more times. I've drank all my life. Well, as soon as I was old enough to lift 'em up and pour 'em down my throat," he paused and looked at each person in the group individually for a split second.

He looked down at the table and began to speak, "I was celebrating the Bicentennial. 1976. Most of you probably weren't even born yet. I was headed home from the bar out on west Kellogg – it was before they built the elevated highway. So I remember hitting this cat on the way home. Vaguely. Just a little *whump*. It kind of woke me up. I blinked my eyes and shook my head, wondering what a cat was doing on the highway."

His voice was quiet and gravely as if what little time in his life he didn't spend drinking, he spent smoking. Something about his story caused me to listen to each and every word. His calming tone was like the man who does the *Meat it's what's for dinner* commercials. As he sat and stared down at the table, I waited for the rest of his story.

"It was about three in the morning when they woke me up. Four of 'em. They wanted to see my truck. I stumbled to the garage and opened it, not sure why they were so damned worried about a homeless cat. It must have been some special cat. Still today, I remember thinking just that. *Must have been some special cat.* So I opened the garage door. The first one who got to the front of the truck vomited. Right there. He just pushed his hands onto his trouser legs and threw up right there in my garage. I don't really remember what all the rest of 'em said, but when they turned me around to put the handcuffs on me is when I saw his leg. It was kinda under the bumper, caught in my brush guard," he hesitated and wiped the tears from his face.

The room was silent. As he rubbed his eyes with his index fingers, he cleared his throat. After a short moment of silence, he continued.

"You see, the cat I hit wasn't a cat. It was a kid. He was nineteen. He was trying to change the tire on his truck was what they told me in court. He was going home to his wife and their newborn baby. He worked the night shift at the diner that used to sit at the intersection of Edgemoor and Kellogg. The other day would have been his birthday. I woke up drunk the next morning. The sixth of June. Tough thing to forget, killing someone. I suppose all things considered, we probably ain't supposed to forget. Probably ain't so much God's will to let us to. Well, that's all I got. Hope it helps one of ya make it out of this disease alive."

He pulled a handkerchief from his pocket and blew his nose. Several people wiped tears from their eyes. I raised my hand to my mouth and nibbled the tips of my fingernails. I've always been fascinated with what we remember and what our mind chooses to set aside as either useless or unworthy of recollection at a later date. Without a doubt, Bill's story would stick with me for a lifetime. I moved my hand to my chin and stared at him blankly as I thought of his misfortune.

KARTER

Often, words come out of my mouth before my mind has time to apply the brakes. Because most of my thoughts are good, it's generally not a problem. *Generally.* Inevitably, there are times after I've spoken when I wish I would have been able to catch myself, bite my lip, and prevent me or others from being embarrassed.

"What was his name?" I asked, "the nineteen year old boy?"

All eyes shifted to me. Maybe I shouldn't have asked. It didn't seem inappropriate at the time, but as everyone stared I wondered about the consensus of the group. He lowered his hand from his face and leaned forward in his chair as he stuffed the handkerchief into his pants pocket. He sniffed again loudly and narrowed his gaze as his eyes focused on mine.

"You know Karter, that's what's strange. I can remember the day it happened like it was yesterday. I can remember the name on the officer's uniform who handcuffed me. I recall the smell of the vomit. Hell, it's *still* stuck in my nose. But now? Now I can't remember his name. Can't really say when it was I forgot, but I did. Don't rightly know if it's a good thing or a bad thing, but it's the truth. Any more, he's just become a date. June 6, 1976," he sighed as he shook his head slightly.

I pursed my lips and stared at the basket, frustrated he was incapable of remembering the name of the boy. I wanted to know who he was, what his name was, and what his wife and son thought about everything. How their lives were affected by the events of that one night in 1976 when everything changed for them. Without a name, it seemed as if it didn't even matter. It was just some bullshit story from some bullshit old man in a bullshit room of a bullshit drug treatment program.

Twenty-seven more days and this nightmare would be over. I picked the remaining polish from my authority finger with my thumbnail as I became more frustrated at Bill's lack of memory. As I blew the flakes of polish from the edge of the table, I nodded my head and grinned.

When this nightmare ends, I'll paint all twenty-eight days on a new canvas.

Today will be a pile of bullshit.

And a face with no name.

JAK

After fractionally more than twenty years in the Navy, I received exactly what I wanted; retirement. Now my days felt empty and my life seemed meaningless. In a sense, I'd ridden a roller coaster for the last two decades, and now expected to be satisfied with standing on the ground. Without a doubt, some positions in the military are without any degree of excitement. Being deployed as an active duty Navy SEAL was not one of those positions. I suspected the feelings of worthlessness could be compared to the countless police who retired and eventually committed suicide over feelings of either guilt or deep depression. Navy SEALS were no exception, and especially if they were exposed to the level of combat I was exposed to. Post-Traumatic Stress Disorder and suicide went hand in hand for far too many military veterans. Although I didn't want to become a statistic, the possibility was a little too close to reality.

I was far from deeply depressed, but the last three days away from my SEAL Team seemed like another lifetime altogether. As I accelerated to merge into traffic, I quickly realized there was a motorcycle stalled in the center of the lane in front of me. When I instinctively stomped on the brake pedal, the right rear tire locked up and screeched on the pavement until the truck came to a stop.

The woman kneeling in front of the motorcycle quickly turned and extended her middle finger in the air as she stood. A few purple highlights stood out in clear contrast to the more prominent brown color of her hair. A helmet hung from the left handlebar of the bike, and what appeared to be a small tool kit was unrolled beside the front tire. The thighs of the faded jeans she wore were almost worn through. A Ramones tee shirt and a pair of canvas sneakers blended appropriately with the colorful tattoos on her right arm. As I released the brake and carefully pulled my truck to the side, I pushed the button to activate the emergency flashers.

"Sorry about the brake locking up," I said as I got out of the truck.

"If you'd have hit my bike, I'd be beating your big ass about now," she said as she kneeled down began to gather her tools.

"Fair enough," I shrugged.

"I saw you as soon as I came around the corner. The truck hasn't been driven for years, probably needs to have the brakes checked. My name's Jak. Need some help?" I asked as I stepped toward the motorcycle.

"Battery's dead. Looks like I need a new voltage regulator," she responded as she stood.

I turned and admired the motorcycle. I didn't much care for motorcycles, but it was a beautiful bike. Everything that wasn't covered in glossy black paint was chromed. As she walked around the other side of the bike, she appeared to be sizing me up for a fight.

"Need a ride somewhere?" I asked.

"I'm not leaving it here," she snapped as she pointed toward the cars entering the highway.

"Well," I hesitated as I turned toward the truck.

"We can load it in the bed of the truck. I've got some tie-down straps in the back."

"You got any ramps?" she raised her eyebrows and pushed her fingers into her back pockets.

"No, but we shouldn't need them. Together we can lift the front tire into the bed, you can get in, and I'll lift the rear in by myself," I said confidently.

"It's a full size Harley Softail. It weighs seven fifty," she chuckled.

"Well, it's worth a try," I shrugged.

"Better not scratch it. I'm Karter," she said as she reached over the bike.

Her hand was covered in grease, paint, and tattoos. Without hesitation, I took her hand in mine and shook it firmly. If she was nothing else, she was an interesting woman. She looked as if she spent a considerable amount of time in the sun, probably on her bike. It was difficult to tell her age due to the dark color of her tanned skin, but my guess was somewhere in her latter twenties.

"I'm Jak," I said as we shook.

"Yeah, you said that already. I heard you the first time," she nodded as she released my hand.

She swiftly kicked the kick-stand and began pushing the bike toward the rear of the truck.

"I got it, this isn't the first time I've had to push this fucker somewhere," she said as I tried to help her push the bike backward.

"Fair enough," I said as I released the seat from my grasp and smiled.

"You said that earlier. *Fair enough.* Quite a vocabulary you have, Jak," she smiled as she brought the bike to a stop alongside the rear of the truck.

In twenty years of travels, I'd been to more countries than I could ever count, and encountered no less than a million people. I had never, however, been exposed to any woman more brash than Karter. I smiled and rolled my eyes as she positioned the bike in the center of the truck's bumper.

"Just hop in the bed and steady the handlebars," I said as I lowered the tailgate.

"Fair enough," she responded.

I turned to face her and smiled. As she jumped into the bed of the truck, I noticed the knife clipped to her right jeans pocket. Although many people in recent years carried knives, very few chose one worth actually using. She, on the other hand, had selected one worthy of combat. One *I* would have chosen.

"*Benchmade*. Nice choice," I nodded as I pulled upward on the handlebars.

"Thanks for noticing. Not much sense in carrying some cheap fucker from Wal-Mart. Anything worth doing is worth doing right," she said as he bent over and reached for the handlebars.

"I agree," I responded.

A *Benchmade* folding combat style knife would cost a civilian roughly three hundred dollars. When a similar but certainly less effective copy could be purchased for one tenth the cost, the few who chose to carry such a blade generally did so for a reason. A gorgeous Harley riding, tattooed, combat knife carrying woman covered in miscellaneous colors of paint and grease. If Karter was doing nothing else, she was capturing my interest.

I needed to know more.

As soon as the rear tire of the bike entered the bed of the truck, she grinned as if she wondered all along whether or not I could have actually lifted it.

"So you're more than just big and sexy. You're actually useful, Jak. You hold it steady, and I'll strap it down," she said as she straightened the handlebars.

She thinks I'm sexy.

Well, Karter, the feeling is mutual.

"Fair enough," I chuckled.

Maybe retirement wouldn't be so bad after all.

KARTER

I've never really been attracted to a man without knowing an awful lot about him. To me, looks aren't everything. They certainly help, but without a personality and a fascinating background, an attractive man is nothing more than a turd sprinkled in powdered sugar.

Underneath, a turd will always remain.

For what reason I wasn't sure, but Jak could have been the biggest, stinkiest, most repulsive turd ever, and I doubt it would have mattered. I'd never been in the presence of a man who immediately captured my attention and kept it. He could have stood up, slapped me, and told me to fuck off and I'm afraid I would have followed him home. As little time as we'd spent together, I knew one thing for sure.

Jak made me feel like a carefree little girl.

"Worst bike wreck as a kid?" I asked.

He choked on his salad as he erupted into laughter, "This is a good one."

He lifted his hand to his mouth and touched his two front teeth with his index finger, "See these?"

I narrowed my gaze and admired the whitest teeth I'd ever seen in a man's mouth, "Your teeth?"

"These two. My two front teeth," he tapped the tip of his finger against them.

KARTER

"Okay?" I looked down at my plate as if I was interested in the salad it contained.

I wasn't. Not at all.

I wanted to stare at him and find an imperfection. He looked like a muscular version of David Beckham. I was having a difficult time *not* staring. I tried to center my mouth over my plate just in case I drooled. As he began to speak, he started laughing again. As soon he caught his breath he lowered his fork onto his plate and wiped his hands on the napkin neatly positioned on his thigh.

No matter what he says or does, stare at your plate, Karter. Do not fuck this up.

"I was riding behind my best friend. This cute girl crossed the street. I think I was twelve. It was summertime and she was wearing shorts and a cute tangerine colored top, but it was really her hair that caught my attention," he paused and began lightly chuckling.

"Her hair?" I said without looking up.

"Yes. She had beautiful hair. Dark brown, similar to yours," he paused.

"Fair enough," I sighed.

Damn it, Karter. He's going to get annoyed and you'll never see him again. Settle down. Breathe. Just breathe.

"You're never going to let that go, are you?" he chuckled.

"So I stared at her as she crossed the street. My buddy yelling at me caused me to look back in his direction, but it was too late. I hit a telephone pole and my mouth smacked the handlebars. Knocked out my two front teeth. Well, it snapped them off. They're fake," he tapped them again with the tip of his finger.

I stared at my salad and counted the remaining pieces of chicken.

Nine. I wondered how many it had when I started. As he began to speak again, I tried not to look up. After what appeared to be an eternity, I gave in and admired his dimples as he grinned.

"Nice," I said as I took another precursory glance at his perfect smile.

I picked up my fork and stirred through my salad. As I attempted to find a cranberry, I wondered how old he thought I might be. He was obviously older than I was, and I didn't care. I felt if we got to know each other a little more my age might not matter to him. If he became attracted to me, truly attracted to me, he wouldn't care. If I didn't offer, hopefully he wouldn't ask. With his boyish smile and smooth skin, I guessed he was probably in his early thirties.

"Let's hear it," he said.

I looked up and smiled. His hands rested on the bottom of his chin. I glanced down at his plate. He had almost the same amount of salad as I did. I had been picking at my meal trying to make our lunch last as long as possible.

Maybe he enjoys this as much as I do.

"Mine didn't knock out any teeth or leave any scars, but it broke my collar bone," I paused and tapped my right shoulder.

"Continue," he said softly.

His eyes all but demanded I stare into them, but I didn't dare. Jak was dangerous, at least for me. Something about an older man attracted me much more than a younger, less experienced, less tactful boy. The difference between thirty-one and twenty-one was the difference between right and wrong. His size, strength, and handsome looks made me uncomfortably comfortable. As I thought of him lifting my bike into the back of the truck, I smiled and continued.

KARTER

"I built a ramp out of plywood and two by fours. In hindsight, I should have used two by sixes. In life's major fuck ups, there's always a retrospective glance where remorse washes over us. Mine revealed a poor lumber choice. Anyway, I built a ramp outside of town by the river in a pasture. My friend had a Suburban, and I always wanted to jump a Suburban on my bike, so we pulled it along the front of the ramp," I hesitated and shook my head at the thought of my failed jump.

"Wait a minute. A Suburban? Like a Chevy Suburban? The SUV?" he asked.

I nodded my head, "You got it."

Were you jumping it sideways or lengthways?" he asked.

"Lengthways. Shit anyone could make it sideways," I responded, half irritated he would think I was interested in the easy way out of anything.

"A Suburban's eighteen feet four inches in length," he chuckled.

"Probably. But you know what?" I asked.

He raised his eyebrows, "What?"

"What's scary is you know that. The length of a Suburban," I laughed.

He looked somewhat embarrassed. I reminded myself to attempt keeping my mouth shut for the remainder of our lunch meeting. The fact he helped me get my bike to the Harley dealer and waited until I got it running was far more than I would have ever expected from a person passing by. One advantage of living in the Midwest, I suppose. The meal was my idea, and a last ditch effort to spend a little more time with him. Hopefully my charm and good looks would lure him into asking for my phone number.

"I'm full of useless information," he smiled.

"Okay. So, down the ramp as fast as I could go and I hauled ass up the other side. As soon as my front tire got to the top of the ramp, I heard a *snap*. The ramp collapsed. Fucking two by fours couldn't hold that much downforce. My bike shot in the air like a rocket, flipped half way over, and I landed on my head and shoulders. My right clavicle ended up cracked. It hurt like hell," I looked down and began to pick at my salad again.

"How far did you make it?" he laughed.

I looked up from my salad and smiled, "Half way."

"Not bad," he grinned.

I sat staring at my salad, relieved he didn't ask when it happened or how old I was. Had he, I would have felt a need to tell a lie. I really wanted to see him again, and I didn't want my age to come into play. Luckily, I just turned twenty-one years old and was able to legally go into bars and clubs. If we would have met six weeks prior and he invited me out to a club, I couldn't have gone. Thank God for the treatment program keeping me off the streets.

"So, how old…"

"Excuse me?" I stammered, not quite hearing the end of his question.

"Your age," he rubbed his chin and appeared to look through me.

Son of a fucking bitch, seriously? I'm twenty-one and I think you're gorgeous, interesting, sexy and for some fucking reason you make me comfortable. I don't care how old you are and I want you to take off your clothes.

At least your shirt.

"How old were you when it happened?"

"Huh?"

"When you broke your clavicle?"

KARTER

"Oh, twelve. I think I was twelve," I lied.

He nodded his head and looked down at his plate. He picked up his fork and stirred through his salad. Slowly he looked up. As our eyes made contact, he smiled.

Fuck, dude. Please don't ask me how long ago it was.

"I've got to be honest," he sighed.

About what?

Fuck, can't we just enjoy this?

You're married, aren't you?

"I've been picking through my lettuce for an hour. I really don't want this to end. I haven't had this much fun in years. Not to sound like one of life's inexperienced assholes slinging cliché remarks, but..." he paused and stared into my eyes.

Thank fucking God.

"I've never felt such an immediate interest in someone before," he smiled, revealing his dimples.

I want you to pick me up and hold me off the floor so my legs dangle.

"That's not too cliché. Kind of, but not bad," I smiled.

Jesus, Karter. Tell him how you feel.

"Well it's true. Karter, you interest me. Let's do this again," he sighed.

"I want you to pick me up and let my legs dangle."

"Say again?" his scrunched his brow and looked confused.

Did I actually say that? Like out loud?

I sat and did my best to act like I didn't hear him.

"Did you say you wanted me to pick you up?" he asked.

I shrugged my shoulders and smiled, "Maybe."

"Well, we've made great progress for five hours," he said as he stood from his seat.

"How so?"

Seeing him stand over me was intimidating and comforting both. He was built like an athlete. Not huge like a pro football player, but extremely muscular and physically fit in appearance. His chest was massive and the muscles in his arms flexed every time he moved them. As he walked around the table I sat and stared.

"Well, five hours ago you told me you were going to beat my ass. Now you want me to pick you up from the floor and let your legs dangle. I'd say that's pretty good progress. Are you going to stand up?"

I felt hypnotized. I stood from my seat. As he hugged me, he lifted me from my feet with ease. My legs dangling and my feet six inches from the floor, I buried my face against his shoulder and my chest pressed to his. Having known Jak all of five hours, and seeing where my mind had allowed me to comfortably go, I wondered what changes a little more time would bring. I lifted my head from his shoulder and positioned my mouth a few inches from his ear.

"So you want my number?" I whispered.

"Reach into my back pocket and pull out my phone. Type your name and number into it, Karter," he responded.

I immediately shoved my hand deeply into his pocket.

Yeah, this man is going to be trouble for me.

Big trouble.

JAK

A short marriage early in my military career didn't prohibit me from trusting women, but it had prevented me from actively pursuing them afterward. Due to long periods of time away from home during deployments, to be a wife of a Navy SEAL was difficult and required an extremely independent woman. Although I believed her to be capable of loyalty during my time away, I was incorrect.

A surprise visit to the United States ended up being just that. *A big surprise*. Her repeated attempts to lure me away from the home as soon as I had arrived raised doubt, but the breathing I heard from our bedroom was the dead giveaway. After pulling him from the closet and beating him senseless, I left. Feeling foolish for having made the decision to allow myself to feel emotion in the first place, I promptly filed for a divorce. Incapable of devoting one hundred percent mentally and emotionally to the SEAL missions which immediately followed convinced me a Navy SEAL had no business in any form of relationship or feeling any degree of attachment to a woman whatsoever.

I should have listened when they warned me.

If your SEAL Team wanted you to have a wife, they would have issued you one.

With the military now behind me and feeling as if my emotional nerve endings were exposed to Karter, I could see no real risk. If things between us did not work out, I only subjected myself to harm. Proceeding along this path with her did not place the military, my teammates, or the mission at risk - only me. My emotional progress was instrumental to my success as a civilian. Beginning my new life in a different city and including a woman and the associated emotions would be typical. Naturally, we migrate toward members of the opposite sex. Seeking what we are unable to achieve alone, we hope for compassion, understanding, loyalty, and love.

I found it to be extremely rewarding being in Karter's presence. Something about her allowed me to immediately become relaxed. I felt comfortable with her. I was warned in my briefing prior to retirement I may feel depressed and uneasy, and to seek mental health at the Veteran's Administration if necessary. With Karter, my feeling was the exact opposite. I felt different than I had ever felt in the presence of anyone. In actuality, she scared me.

Graduating high school and immediately spending more than twenty years in the military left me no time to live a common life or deal with typical emotions. To become effective in combat, a SEAL must be able to turn off emotional attachments. Therefore, I had zero experience in feeling emotion and acting upon it. My entire military career was spent without sentiment. I had been a stone-faced killer for almost two decades. To think a person could change from being a trained killer on Friday to compassionate civilian on Monday would be ludicrous.

Based on my lack of experience on allowing myself to feel or act upon emotions, I now felt as if I was now a thirty-eight year old high school kid. I couldn't decide if Karter was filling a void as an individual or by the mere design of simply being a woman. Would I have been attracted to *any* woman who exposed herself to me, or was Karter truly special? Finding the answer on an absolute level would be impossible. I knew one thing for certain; Karter caused me to feel emotion. As I stood beside the running track at a local high school, I felt as if I couldn't breathe. It wasn't the three miles I had run which had me breathless.

It was Karter's absence.

I didn't *want* to see her.

I felt I *needed* to.

Not necessarily feeling uneasy, but feeling differently than I was accustomed to, I recalled my discussion with Commander Warrenson on my last day in the Navy.

"For the last twenty years, you've been told what to do - when to eat, what to eat, where to go and where not to go. You've lived your respective life against the clock; one split-second separates life from death on a mission. You're no longer on a mission. Kennedy. My best advice is this; enjoy doing whatever you want whenever you want. Open up emotionally, and allow yourself to feel. You're going to be free when you leave here, and you've paid a high price for it. Enjoy it."

Instinctively I glanced at my watch.

He shook his head and did his best to smile.

"Here in about two minutes, you'll no longer be Kennedy. You'll leave here as Jak," he looked up at the clock on the wall.

As the minute hand snapped into position, he smiled, "Lose your watch and enjoy life, Jak."

I stretched my legs and began walking to the small maintenance building between the track and the school. As soon as I arrived in town, I looked for a private place to run. The new high school north of the city seemed a logical place, as it was somewhat secluded and school was out for the summer. In my initial survey of the facility, an elderly maintenance man approached me on a golf cart. Although his black skin made it difficult at first, my attentive nature allowed me to notice the outline of a tattoo on his forearm - an eagle, globe, and anchor. He was a former Marine, and in a sense, a military brother. Without reservation, he gave me permission to run on the track for the summer months during the school's recess from classes. Generations separated us, but we would always have the common bond of war and the recovery associated with attempting to become human again. As I walked around the corner of the building, I noticed the door to the building was open. Before I stepped into the opening, his voice echoed through the small concrete facility.

"How many miles this morning, Jak?"

I stepped remaining distance to the doorway and walked inside, "Your old ears work well, Oscar. I ran three. I couldn't stay focused, so I stopped. How's your day progressing?"

He turned from the work bench, revealing a disassembled pump on the table in front of him, "We're gonna get off to a fucked up start young man, you keep calling me old. And I couldn't be any better unless I was twins. What's on your mind?"

Oscar was somewhere close to seventy years old, bald, and still resembled the Marine he once was. Marines claim once they're a Marine they're always a Marine, and Oscar was certainly no exception. He seemed to be in great health, and appeared to be very physically fit. Short of his own admittance of his age and the grey goatee beard he wore, I would have never guessed him to be seventy years old.

I grinned and responded, "I've got one quick question, and I'll get out of your hair."

He walked to the golf cart and sat on the edge of the fender, "I know you ain't a dumb man Jak, so I'm gonna go on and just guess you's blind. I ain't got no hair. What's ailin' ya?"

"When you got back, how long was it before you were in a relationship?"

He looked up at the ceiling as if recalling past memories and smiled. As he leaned away from the golf cart and slowly walked my direction, he began to chuckle, "Hell Jak, I was married when I left for Viet Nam. I had a young 'un. I was twenty-eight when I got shot in 1969. And when I got back I went home and tried to act like nothin' happened. Now what's really ailin' ya?"

"I met a girl," I sighed.

"I sure don't see that as a *problem*. Sounds like the man upstairs might be lookin' after ya," he grinned and pointed his index finger in the air.

I nodded my head, "Thanks Oscar. Well, I'll see you tomorrow."

He pressed his hands into his hips and widened his eyes, "Hold up, lightnin'. That's what's wrong with your generation. You're always in a damned hurry. So, you met a girl. What's troublin' ya about it?"

Feeling somewhat embarrassed, I responded truthfully, "I already feel as if I *need* her. It's almost like I've known her for years, but we just met."

He leaned into the fender of the golf cart and grinned, "Ain't no shame in that, Jak. Now, you scared you're gonna fuck it up or are you thinkin' she's gonna hurt ya? Which one?"

I thought about what he asked. I really didn't know the answer. I wasn't sure it was either I was afraid of. More accurately, I feared what I felt was an unnatural attraction based on the amount of time I had known Karter. I opted to respond with a brief but accurate answer.

I bent down, touched my toes, and responded as I stood, "I'm afraid it's too early for me to feel like this."

"Too early? Shit, feelin's ain't got a time clock, Jak. An' if you're worried about *you*, lemme tell ya somethin'. I was over there a little better'n two years. Two years of hell, fo' sho'. When I come back, I was like a dried out sponge. I sucked up everything what got close to me. Sights, sounds, food, feelin's - I just sucked 'em up," he leaned forward and stood from the golf cart's fender as he began to laugh.

"I was prob'ly back a week at the time. I walked up to this tree and for some reason I just stared at it. I looked up in it and I remember smilin'. She was a biggun, prob'ly a forty footer. An' I just climbed that sum bitch. Hell, I was damned near thirty years old, an' I climbed a tree. You wanna know why?"

I smiled and nodded my head, "Yes sir."

"Because I could," he grinned.

He pulled a plastic tipped cigar from his pocket and waved it at me as he spoke, "War dries us out Jak. Two years dried me right up. Hell, you been at it for damned near twenty, you're drier'n a popcorn fart. Go absorb some of what God intended for ya to. And don't fuss about lettin' your heart open up. If she's a good girl for ya, you'll heart'll know it."

He lifted the cigar to his mouth and chewed on the tip as if satisfied he made had his point. As I considered his comments, he narrowed his eyes and pulled the cigar from his mouth. He pointed the tip in my direction and smiled as he nodded his head sharply, "And if she was bad, we wouldn't be havin' this talk now would we?"

I smiled and shook my head, "No sir."

He turned and slowly walked toward the bench. After what appeared to be a short recollection of where he was when I disturbed him, he reached down, picked up the electric motor from the pump and set it aside. For an instant he stood motionless.

He looked over his right shoulder. The cigar still dangled from his lips, "Go climb that tree, Jak."

I nodded my head and smiled, "Thanks Oscar. I'll be seeing you."

"Not if I see you first," he chuckled.

I bent down, retied my shoes and jogged to the parking lot. The thought of possibly seeing Karter filled my mind as I unlocked the truck and retrieved my phone from my gym bag. Still standing outside the truck, I swiped the screen of my phone. Upon opening the text screen, I smiled. One lone text message was all I had received. It was all I needed. Anxiously, I opened the message.

Karter Wilson: I can't paint and I don't want to ride. All I can think about is you. Dude, what the fuck did you do to me?

I stared at the screen, knowing what I wanted to say, but feeling as if I shouldn't send a message which would allow her to perceive me as weak or needy.

Fuck it, Jak. Be honest with this girl. Be honest with yourself. Tell her what you're thinking. Then, she'll know exactly how you feel. If she's still interested it'll be for all the right reasons.

I inhaled, studied at the screen for a second, and typed a brief but heartfelt response.

I feel the same way.

I tossed the phone onto the top of my bag and climbed into the seat of the truck. After a shower and change of clothes, I'd be ready for a new day of relaxation. As I pushed the key into the ignition, my phone beeped. I reached for it and immediately swiped my thumb across the screen as I raised it to my chest.

KARTER

Karter Wilson: I'm dying a slow miserable death. End the fucking pain. Come over, pick me up, and then leave if you have to. But come pick me up. Mosley Street Apts. #211.

Uncertain if she meant to pick her up from her apartment and take her somewhere or lift her from her feet again, I reread the message. Still unclear and not wanting to make any assumptions, I typed a universal response.

I'm in PT gear and need to shower.

I read my message. Dissatisfied with the military reference, I erased it and retyped another message.

I just got done running and I'm in shorts and a tee shirt. Give me an hour.

I pressed send.

I tossed my phone onto my gym bag. As I gripped the key with my thumb and forefinger, the phone beeped. I shook my head and smiled as I lifted it from the bag and cleared the screen.

*Karter Wilson: An hour? Fuck that. Did you not read my first message? I'm dying. Like DYING. I'm dressed inappropriately as well. Come as you are. Make it quick. *collapses to floor and drops phone**

I laughed audibly and shook my head. Damn, this girl seemed to be exactly what I needed. If nothing else, she would keep me on my toes. I looked down at my sweaty shorts and pressed my hand against the chest of my tee shirt. *Wet.*

If she's truly dying I suppose it's my solemn duty to attempt to save her.

I typed a quick response and pressed send.

En route. ETA fifteen minutes.

I tossed my phone onto the bag and started the truck. As I backed away from the parking stall, my phone beeped. I shook my head and rolled my eyes. After I stopped the truck and pushed the gear shifter into park, I picked up the phone and glanced at the screen.

Karter Wilson: *coughs* Hurry. I'll be on the floor. *coughs again* If I appear lifeless, it's your fucking fault. Perform CPR as necessary. *crawls and unlocks door*

As I drove toward downtown, I found it odd out of everything we had discussed the previous day, we neglected our jobs. Although I purposely didn't ask her of hers, she offered the fact she painted. At the time I had no idea if it was a full-time job or a hobby. The fact Karter now mentioned she couldn't paint and was home during the work day led me to believe it may be her job.

I was reluctant to offer my employment history because I didn't want her to determine my age - at least not yet. If she was in her latter twenties as I suspected, I was at least ten years her senior. If we continued along the same path, it would stand to reason after six months of further developing attractions toward one another, age would never become an issue. I felt if she provided me an opportunity to show her who I was and how I was capable of caring for her, she'd accept my age as being just what it was - a mere number.

As I exited the highway into downtown, I chuckled at applying the government's position on gays in the military to our age difference.

Don't ask - don't tell.

It had been a little more than twenty years since I spent any time in Wichita, but it didn't matter much. The downtown area remained unchanged for the most part. I was well aware of where her apartment building was located as I had viewed them when I arrived to town a matter of a few days prior. Whether it would prove to be a blessing or a curse was yet to be determined, but I lived three short blocks from her location.

I had grown up in a small town thirty miles outside of Wichita, and had gone to school there from kindergarten to my senior year in high school. During my initial training, my mother relocated to Wichita and remained there. This made my selection of a location to retire rather easy. I had no intent of visiting my home town or anyone in it, and as far as I was concerned if I lived in a city of almost half a million people, no one would know or recognize me. In a sense, I was obtaining a fresh start in a new city.

I parked my truck in the street outside her apartment building. After a precursory glance in the rearview mirror, I decided it really didn't matter. I couldn't change anything if I wanted to. I was without any cologne, brush, comb, or clean clothes. I had no idea my morning would have eventually led me to Karter's apartment. Surprisingly, I felt comfortable seeing her covered in sweat and dressed in my PT gear.

As I knocked on the door of her apartment the sound from inside resembled a herd of elephants being assembled for a circus. Eventually, the door opened and Karter stood before me dressed in paint covered sweats, canvas sneakers, a Rolling Stones tee shirt, and a beanie. The shirt appeared to be something she had used for years, as it was covered in both wet and dry paint. The beanie rested atop her head more as an adornment than a necessity. As she swung the door open she waved her free arm toward the ridiculously colorful apartment.

"Mi casa, su casa," she said softly as she waved her arm.

I quickly surveyed the very large open area and couldn't help but grin at the furnishings and her choice of decorative accents. Three unmatched sofas sat in the front room, but they worked very well together. Various paintings littered the walls; most I now assumed were the result of her mind's creative talent. Each wall was painted a different color, all bright and colorful. In the far corner sat a wooden trunk with an old glass screened television lying on its side. Numerous light fixtures hung from the ceiling, all at different elevations. After a split second inventory, I turned to her and smiled.

"Su casa es muy colorido. Me gusta su elección de ropa, eres muy linda," I responded without thinking.

She raised one eyebrow, "Huh?"

The look on her face was clear. She didn't speak Spanish. I asked anyway, "You don't speak Spanish?"

"Negative Ghostrider," she said flatly.

"What the fuck did you say?" she asked as she released the door.

"I said your home is very colorful, and you look cute. Well, I actually said I like your choice of clothes and you look cute," I said as I stepped past her.

"Me or the clothes?" she asked the instant I finished speaking.

"Both. Your tee shirt choices are great. I've seen two so far, and I like them both. Your sweats are, well," I paused and looked down at her skin tight sweats which were cut off right below her knees.

Her calves were tan and smooth. She didn't appear overly athletic nor did she seem out of shape. I guessed her to have naturally good genes which afforded her a well put together physique of average proportions. As I found myself lost in my admiration of her legs, she snapped her fingers loudly.

She wagged her hand in the air in front of her face, "Dude, snap out of it. I'll change the cocksucker's if you don't like 'em. Hold please."

She no more than finished speaking and bounced through the apartment like a deer chasing after a mate. Swiftly, she disappeared into an open rear bedroom. After a few seconds of grunting and what I assumed was rustling through her available clothes, she stepped into the opening of the bedroom door.

She raised her arms parallel with the floor and motioned toward her torso with her index fingers, "Tadahhh."

She stood in the doorway wearing a relatively paint free Bod Dylan tee shirt, shorts with more holes than actual available material, and a curved bill baseball style cap with the phrase *Fuck Off* stenciled across the front of the crown. Now barefoot, she performed a slow pirouette in the doorway, revealing a fabulously rounded ass, some of which was exposed by the six inch rip in the rear of her jean shorts immediately below her left butt cheek.

I shook my head in disbelief. The entire event, from my comment to her reappearance didn't take thirty seconds.

She frowned, "No likey?"

"Actually, I loved what you were wearing."

As I paused she quickly turned toward the room.

"Stop!" I said sternly.

Having realized the military man in me was coming out, I softened my tone, "But I like what you're wearing now more."

"I love this hat. It keeps the creeps away," she smiled as she turned and sauntered into the living room area.

"So, you paint?" I asked as I admired the numerous paintings.

"We've been over this already, Jak," she snapped as she stepped over the back of the largest couch in the room.

I walked to the couch and lowered myself onto the cushion at the opposite end, "Well, I wasn't sure if it was a hobby or a profession. I guess I still don't know, but it appears you're a very talented woman."

She pressed her back into the arm of the couch and widened her eyes, "So is this how we're going to do it now?"

"Excuse me?" I asked.

She raised her index finger and pulled down on her lower lip, "Me sitting on this end and you on the other. The only way we could be further apart is if you sat in the street. Do you want to sit in the street, Jak?"

I shrugged my shoulders lightly, "No, I..."

"Then scoot the fuck down here. Jesus, Jak. Did you forget what I said? I'm dying. D. Y. I. N. G.," she released her lip and slumped into the lower cushion of the couch.

I smiled and stood from the end of the couch. As I stepped toward her she looked up, grinned, and batted her eyes repeatedly. As I walked her direction, I stared at her obsessively. Not watching where I was walking, I became tangled in newspapers which littered the floor in front of the couch and stumbled. I looked down at the pile of old papers and shook my head.

"Sorry, I read the obituaries. It's the only part I read. I like knowing the names of people who die. I do it every morning when the paper comes," she said as she kicked the newspapers aside.

I shook my head lightly as I stood over her and admired her beauty.

"I like it that you're taller than me. I hate short guys. Actually I hate guys, period. All guys. I suppose we just as well go over this now," she sighed.

I sat down beside her feet and turned to face her. Now almost lying flat on the couch, she raised her head and rested her cheek in her palm.

KARTER

Upon meeting a person, it's difficult to know for certain if the actions and expressed personality of a person are genuine or an act. Without a doubt, sometimes it's a combination of both. Strangely, I felt with Karter what I witnessed was exactly who she was. I cocked one eyebrow comically, "All guys? And go over what?"

She sat up slightly and pushed her feet under my right thigh, "Okay here's the deal. I hate men. I always have. It hasn't prevented me from being in relationships, but it's prevented me from lasting for any period of time. All men are turds and I use them when I need to. Never for money and never for material things, but I've used a few for sex."

"A woman has her sexual needs. I've fucked a handful of dudes and eventually they fuck me over. But don't mistake what I'm telling you. I'm no slut, and I'm not an easy lay, Jak." she paused and sat up a little more.

"Men have no depth. They have no appreciation. They want laid, and that's it. I'm a complex person, Jak. I'm not high maintenance in a sense of fashion or finance, but my mind goes a million miles an hour and the world spins slowly. I can't slow it down, I've tried. So, what you're seeing? This girl covered in paint and wearing the *Fuck Off* hat? This is me. I'd be doing this and wearing these same clothes at some point in time if you weren't here. I might do something eventually to piss you off, but I'll never do anything intentionally to impress you. It's not how I roll," she hesitated and straightened her knees, pushing her feet further under my thigh.

"Well, I like it that..."

"I wasn't done," she said as she raised her index finger in the air.

"Fair enough," I chuckled.

She rolled her eyes and lowered her hand to her chin.

"So I meet guys and eventually I settle for one and whatever. You know the deal. But I've never felt like they cared, or I cared, or that there was a real attachment. Nothing ever lasts longer than a few months. Maybe three. But in *here*," she rubbed her hand from her waist to her neck.

"In here, I feel nothing. I never have. Not one time. Not fucking once. I'm not shitting you, Jak. Not one fucking time have I felt anything in here," she continued to rub her hand up and down her torso.

I nodded my head and waited as patiently as I could for the rest of the story she planned to tell. What I hoped to hear was that she felt the same way I felt - an extremely strong attraction for merely having met someone and really knowing nothing about them. I struggled after we had eaten with whether or not it was simply a fascination, but settled on it truly being an attraction. I realized I preferred to be in Karter's presence - and for me - having the desire alone was enough to cause me to believe it was an attraction.

"Now this may scare you or it might excite you. Who fucking knows? But I decided last night I was going to tell you the honest truth. My mind tells me things, and not like you're probably thinking. I hear voices in my head - not the devil or dumb shit like that. But my brain talks to me. I think I'm a genius, but some people think I'm crazy. Maybe everyone is like me and I'm the only one with the guts to admit it, I have no idea," she paused and sat up slightly.

"Yesterday after we ate, you picked me up and held me. When you let me down onto the floor my brain decided it liked you. Like a lot. So, I want to see you as much as you want to see me. I don't want to make you uncomfortable and I don't want to freak you out, but I want to be with you as often as possible. I work from my home and sell this shit to a few studios and individuals who are dumb enough to buy them. I'm always here and I'm always available," she hesitated, raised her finger in the air, and took a deep breath.

She hears voices in her head.

Well, she's not alone.

"So, is this the last I'll see of you?" she asked as she pulled her feet out from under my thigh and pressed her back into the arm of the couch.

I extended my arm and gripped her left ankle in my right hand. As I pulled her toward me, she allowed herself to slump into the couch and slide my direction. I raised my leg and positioned her foot under my thigh. Without speaking, she smiled and pushed her right foot beside it. I lowered my leg and pressed her feet into the cushion of the couch. As I slid my hand along the smooth skin of her calf, I smiled.

"I'm afraid not. My brain decided it liked you too."

KARTER

It was 98 degrees and not even noon yet – a typical June day in the Midwest. Sitting at the green light waiting for traffic to inch forward was always a difficult thing for me to do. I rode responsibly, and not doing dumb shit while on my bike was difficult if not sometimes close to impossible. I wanted to twist the throttle and pass each and every car sitting in front of me. Instead, I inched forward and absorbed the sound of *Jimi Hendrix's The Wind Cries Mary* through the earbuds of my iPod and the sweltering heat from the 1340 cc engine between my legs.

Jak and I met on a Monday, and had seen each other every day for the week which followed. Now Saturday, we had agreed to meet for lunch at *Adrian's*, a Mediterranean restaurant on the east side of town. It seemed Jak had as much free time as I did, and although I felt a need to keep my mouth shut about what he may do for a living, part of me wondered. Actually, I wanted to know everything about him.

As traffic opened up, I sped north on Rock road toward the strip mall. By my watch I would be ten minutes early. Not bad for douchebag infused traffic. As I slowed down and changed into the turning lane, I instinctively checked my mirror. As I rolled to a stop, I watched the reflection of a car rapidly approaching behind me.

Slow it down fuck head, you're coming in kinda hot.

I revved the throttle hoping to get his attention. I looked ahead for a break in traffic.

Shit.

I glanced into my mirror.

Double shit.

Through the windshield of the car fast approaching behind me, I could clearly see a man texting on his phone. He appeared to have no idea I was in his lane or even in front of him. After alternating glances between oncoming traffic and the mirror, I decided I had only one option short of allowing him to plow into the back of my bike. I revved the throttle and shot forward between two oncoming cars, launched up the entrance ramp of the strip mall, and came to a stop a few feet before hitting the landscaped area which separated the entrance from the parking lot. As I pulled off my helmet, I heard his tires screech to a stop. Angry and shaking from the adrenaline, I kicked the kickstand of the bike downward and climbed from the seat. I hung my helmet on the left side of the bars, pulled my earbuds from my ears, and turned to wait for him to enter the parking lot.

As he slowly drove up the ramp, I stood in the entrance and waved my arms. He rolled his driver's side window down partially as he approached, still holding his phone in his hand. I rolled my eyes and began screaming as soon as he was beside me.

"You fucktard. You almost hit me," I screamed.

"Well, you're standing here flapping your fucking arms, what do you expect," he responded.

"No, out in the street. I was turning in here. You were fucking texting and I damn near got hit just trying to get out of your way. Pay attention to driving, you piece of shit," I yelled.

"I don't know what you're talking about," he shrugged.

You motherfucker. I ought to cut you.

I reached for my knife and pressed my palm against the outline of the frame in my pocket, "You don't know what I'm talking about because you weren't paying fucking attention. You locked up your brakes to stop, douchebag."

Still holding his phone, he shook it at me through the window, "You mouthy little bitch."

I slapped the phone from his hand, forcing it onto the pavement at my feet. As his jaw dropped, he looked out the window at his phone – now positioned a few inches in front of my right foot. I smiled, kicked his phone across the entrance, and turned toward my bike.

Fucking punk.

"You little cunt," he said as he opened his car door and started to get out.

Cunt?

I pulled my knife from my pocket and flipped the blade out. As it snapped into the locked position, he quickly glanced down at the knife and then up into my eyes. He was considerably bigger outside of the car than he was inside. Standing in front of me it was easy to see he was all of six foot two and probably two hundred plus pounds.

"Get in your car before I stab you so full of God damned holes…"

"What's going on?" a voice said from behind me in a stern tone.

I turned my head slightly to the left.

Shit, it's Jak.

"Jak, this douchebag almost hit me. I was explaining to him the benefit of *not* texting and driving and he called me a cunt," I said as I turned my head to face the walking turd.

"I called you a cunt because you kicked my phone," he rocked his head back and forth as he spoke.

"Whatever, dude. Come pick it up if you're that worried about it," I grinned as I motioned toward his phone.

Jak stepped in front of me and picked up the phone. As he studied the douchebag standing in front of me, he slowly stepped toward him with his arm extended. As the man reached for the phone, he said his parting remarks.

He tossed his head my direction, "Maybe you should keep her on a leash."

In an instantaneous move, Jak dropped the phone, pulled the man's arm toward his chest, and spun him half around. Now with his back at Jak's chest, Jak immediately slammed the man's body against the door of the car and pinned his right arm behind his back. As he lifted the man's arm upward, the douchebag screamed.

Holy shit!

Fuck yes. Jak's a bad-ass.

I fucking knew it.

"Owww. What the fuck?"

Jak moved his face to beside the man's left ear. As he spoke he had a tone of authority to his voice that couldn't be easily dismissed.

"Listen to me and listen carefully," Jak insisted.

Break his arm, Jak. Snap it off and toss it in the street.

"Leashes are for dogs. She's not a dog. She's my fucking wife. Now, when you see her again, and you very well may, her name is Karter. I'm Jak. My best advice to you is this," he paused and looked over his shoulder.

Wife?

He turned and pressed his chin into the man's shoulder as he pulled upward on his arm, "I'm going to release you. Get in your car and go do whatever it was you were planning to before this happened. Look at it as a lesson. I saw what happened from my truck, and you damned near hit her. Don't text and drive, and don't be disrespectful to people. You never know just who it is you might encounter."

"Understood?" Jak asked.

"Yeah," the man grunted.

Jak pulled upward on his arm.

"Fuck dude. *Yeah*," the man screeched.

Jak pulled up on his arm again and with more force.

Oh fuck, that looks painful.

"Yes," the man screamed.

I closed my knife and slid it into my pocket.

Jak released the man's arm, immediately stepped to the side and stood with his knees slightly bent and his hands raised to his chest. The man slowly lowered his arm, rubbed his shoulder, and bent down to pick up his phone. As he stood and opened his car door, he turned and nodded his head once toward Jak. As the man slowly drove away, Jak walked backward slowly between the car and where I stood. Jak continued to watch as the car disappeared into the parking lot, and then turned to face me.

"Move your bike before someone hits it. I'm parked over there," he half demanded as he pointed toward his truck.

I stood and stared, still in awe at what had happened. As he straightened his shirt, I saw a portion of a tattoo under his sleeve – on his bicep. As he tugged his sleeve downward and slowly walked toward his truck, I stared at his ass. He was gorgeous, any idiot could see it. But there was so much more to Jak than his looks. He was a complex person, and I wanted to know more about him. I needed to know everything. As he took the last few steps to his truck, I smiled at his methodical walk.

I want to see you naked, Jak.

I hopped onto my bike, put on my helmet and slowly maneuvered through the parking lot to where Jak was parked. As I parked beside his truck, he opened his door and got out. As I draped the chin strap of my helmet over the handlebars, he stood beside me and shook his head.

"Who taught you how to handle a knife?" he asked.

Oh fuck. Here we go.

Bring the criticism.

"He was a douchbag," I sighed.

"Douchebag or not, he could have slapped that knife from your hand in one stroke. After we eat, we're going to have a lengthy discussion about that fiasco," he snapped.

The thought of upsetting Jak made me feel uneasy. I didn't know if he was actually disappointed, but I knew one thing for certain; I didn't want him to be, at least not with me. Even *considering* how he was feeling was new to me.

I never really cared what anyone thought about me or the choices I made. I had been responsible for my actions since my emancipation from my mother at the age of sixteen. Although I now realize I wasn't always right, I took responsibility for the decisions I made, and suffered the respective consequences when I made mistakes. How an outsider perceived me was never an issue I felt I needed to consider. People who didn't know me may have perceived me as immature, foolish or selfish, but I saw myself as strong and capable. I never felt I needed anyone's approval or opinion to make a decision.

If someone didn't like what I was doing, as far as I was concerned, they could simply fuck off. This attitude and strong willed personality gave me the courage to begin questioning my mother at a very early age. My challenges of her means and methods were not without merit.

As early as I could remember, all I ever wanted my mother to provide me with was an explanation of who my father was. As I got older, what would have sufficed grew smaller and smaller. When I was a young pre-teen girl, I had countless questions and expected many lengthy answers. As I approached my teenage years, a simple explanation of who he was would have satisfied me greatly. Immediately prior to my emancipation, I would have been content if she simply provided me with his name. Knowing my father was dead but not knowing *who* he was never settled well with me.

In the end, my mother and I separated and I changed my name. Despite the fact she lived a mere half hour drive from me, I didn't speak to her. As far as I was concerned, she was no longer my mother.

I followed Jak quietly into the restaurant and tried to come to terms with how I felt. As the waitress seated us, I began to consider the depth of my feelings for Jak could be some form of puppy love. In the more realistic world of Karter Wilson, I wouldn't give half a fuck what Jak thought. But for some reason, at least lately, I wasn't living in my world.

We stepped through the front door into an almost empty restaurant. I glanced around. *Eight booths on the left and ten on the right. Nine tables. Seventy-two plus thirty-six. One hundred and eight.* The restaurant was spacious. Larger spaces allowed me to relax and feel comfortable where smaller more cramped spaces made me extremely uneasy. It was one reason I lived in an apartment with a large open floor plan.

"You can seat yourself. Wherever you like," the waitress smiled.

Jak motioned to a table in the center of the floor and shrugged. I grinned and sat down. As Jak pulled his seat from the table, he surveyed the restaurant. After his quick study, he lowered himself into the seat. I considered the fact he may count things like I do.

Hell, maybe everyone counts things.

"Can I get your drinks coming? Would you like a wine list?" the waitress asked as she placed the menus on the table.

Jak raised his eyebrows and waited for me to respond.

"Unsweetened tea?" I asked.

"Same," Jak smiled.

The waitress nodded and turned away.

"I'm going to wash my hands," I sighed.

Jak nodded and smiled as I stood from my chair.

As I walked back from the bathroom, I noticed Jak watching me admiringly. I smiled at the thought of him being pleased with me. The last thing I wanted to do was start this relationship off on the wrong foot. It seemed all I did was piss people off and drive them out of my life. This was one person I hoped to keep happy. I felt I was willing to make adjustments to me and my attitude if need be. As I pulled my seat from the table, Jak grinned his dimple grin and stared through me.

Keep that shit up and you're going to have to take your clothes off.

"I like it when you smile that smile," I said softly.

"I didn't know I had variations," he said as he raised his hand to his face.

"Well, you have at least two - one with dimples showing and one without. I like the dimples," I nodded.

He covered his mouth with his hand and continued to stare, "You know Karter. I have this thing I do. I study people as they walk. I don't really know why, but I do. I've convinced myself I can tell a lot about a person by how they walk. So, it's become a habit. Your walk?"

He shook his head lightly, "You walk lightly. You almost float. But you do it with authority. Your shoulders tell it all. I love watching you walk."

Dude, just stop. You melted my panties when you picked me up the other day. There's no need to continue.

He lowered his hand from his mouth and reached across the table. I glanced down at his hand. He curled his fingers slowly a few times as if he wanted me to touch his hand. As I reached across the table he cupped my hand in his and smiled. As he placed his other hand around the back side and formed a little hand house, my heart raced.

"When you walk into a room, you fill it. Nothing else exists. There's no room for anything additional. The entire room *becomes* you, Karter. It becomes impossible to pay attention to anything else, because you're not only all that matters, you're all there is," he grinned until his dimples formed.

If you ever leave me, I'm going to stab you in the back. You can't do this to me.

I pulled my hands from his and rubbed them on the thighs of my jeans, "If you fuck me over, I'll kill you. That's not a stupid girl threat. It's a promise, Jak."

"Wow. I'm trying to secure a place in your heart and you threaten me," he chuckled as he leaned into his seat.

"What? Secure a place? You remember what I told you the other day about my brain? My brain deciding it liked you? You remember that Jak?" I asked.

The waitress placed the drinks on the table and smiled, "You ready to order?"

I glanced over my shoulder and gave her my best *go away, bitch* look.

"I'll give you some time," she smiled.

Yeah, do that.

I turned to Jak.

"Yes. I remember. Why?" he asked.

"I'm not trying to be gross. And this isn't an offer. It is what it is, I suppose. But I have never, and I do mean *never*," I paused and shook my head at the thought of discussing the matter.

"I've never been able to have sex without lube. My lady parts don't get wet. They're like fucked up. Medically. Mentally. Who knows. So, the other day when you picked me up? When my feet were dangling in the air?" I raised my eyebrows and waited for him to chew on what I offered so far.

He raised his chin, nodded slightly, and waited for me to continue.

"I got wet. And wet isn't even close to an accurate description. Because I've never been wet Jak, I really couldn't compare it to anything. But if all girls get as wet as you made me, there's no way they can walk around smiling like they do. You want to know what I did after you left?"

He smiled and nodded.

I leaned forward, rested my elbows on the table and my chin against my clenched fists, "I got off my bike, walked back in, and went to the bathroom. I took off my tee shirt and tried to mop up the mess, Jak. My sacred Ramones shirt was covered in pussy juice and I fucking loved it. And, the other day when you pulled me across the couch? That day, Jak? Remember that day?"

He smiled until his dimples formed. He blinked once as he nodded his head.

I raised my chin from my hands and pointed my index finger toward my lap, "Soaked. Fucking soaked. And a minute ago? When you pulled that Kung Fu shit in the parking lot? Guess fucking what?"

He smiled and shrugged.

"Well, I didn't go to the bathroom to wash my fucking hands, Jak. I went and dabbed my pussy until it was *comfortably* wet. I can't make it dry. Not around you. Nope. Just *less wet*. So Jak, now I'm twenty-one years old and I've had my first wet pussy. You want to secure a place in my heart? Alrighty then. You can check that box. You did that a long time ago. What I'm forced to deal with is this; my fucking heart needs you and my brain wants you. So, Jak the mysterious Kung Fu master, leave me. Fuck me over, and I'll stab you. You make my pussy wet, Jak. And I fucking like it," I exhaled loudly and leaned into my seat.

"Fair enough," he smiled.

Are you fucking kidding me?

I leaned forward and slapped my hands against the edge of the table, "Are you fucking kidding me? Fair enough? You need to forget that phrase. You've used it up. *Fair enough?* That's your response?"

He leaned forward and smiled a shitty little smirky smile as he pressed his massive forearms into the table, "I'm not trying to be gross. And this isn't an offer. It is what it is, I suppose. But I have never, and I do mean *never.*"

Did he just repeat what I said earlier word for word?

"I've never had a girl cause my cock to go stiff from simply holding her in my arms. Would you like to know why I chose to sit back down for fifteen minutes after I hugged you the other night?" he cocked one eyebrow slightly and pursed his lips.

KARTER

I attempted to swallow. My face felt hot. I stared at Jak and imagined him with a hard cock. A hard cock which was rightfully mine because I made it hard. I continued to stare as the temperature elevated twenty degrees. I raised my hand to my cheek and began fanning myself frantically.

Is the air conditioner broke in this place?

Feeling somewhat light headed, I looked down at the table and noticed the two glasses of tea. I picked up the one closest to me and took a gulp, "Yes sir. I want to know. Why?"

His lips still pursed, he smirked and lowered his clenched hand to the center of the table. I looked down at his hand. He extended his index finger and curled it toward his palm repeatedly as he slowly leaned into the center of the table.

Here we go again. He's hypnotizing me.

I leaned toward him and attempted to swallow. I rested my elbows on the table and my chin onto my cupped hands. As his face pressed against my cheek, he brushed my hair away from my ear. As I felt his breath against my face, my entire body turned to goosebumps.

Soaked.

As he began to speak, he forced his warm breath into my ear, "Because holding you made me hard as a rock, Karter."

Clean up in aisle seven. Can someone bring me a fucking towel?

"You have no God damned idea what you do to me, do you?" he breathed.

I squeaked.

"When you walked your little walk from the bathroom a minute ago? I watched you. I admired you. And I tried to think of any and everything I could to keep it from happening. But guess what? Guess what you did to me?"

I swallowed heavily and opened my mouth. A puff of hot air passed my lips.

"You made my cock hard again," he paused and quickly scanned the restaurant.

He leaned into me, pressing his cheek to mine and his lips to my ear, "So, Karter Wilson. I have no intent of fucking you over. In fact, I have every intention of making you mine. Mine. Do you understand me, Karter? I don't want to know what it's like to spend another day without you. And that isn't like me at all, but I'm going to proceed with it because you make my otherwise mundane life mean something. Get used to me being around. And if you fuck me over," he paused and leaned away from the table.

He crossed his arms in front of his chest, "That in itself would kill me."

Holy fuck. I want you to smash me against the wall and kiss me, Jak.

"I want you to smash me against the wall and kiss me," I smiled.

He stood from his chair, stepped aside, and pushed it to the table.

I stared up at him and batted my eyes.

He reached into his jeans pocket and removed his wallet. He tossed a few bills on the table. I may or may not have stood up. When I came to my senses, Jak had me pinned against the front door of the restaurant.

And he was kissing me passionately.

JAK

"You see, I can't do that. I can't pull on your sexual strings and have any kind of expectation emotion won't be attached. Everything within us is connected. I've either captured you or I haven't. If I tug on a sexual string I *want* emotion attached," I explained.

"Jak, I'm sorry. I'm lost. I'm frustrated. Fine. Emotion. Sex. Loyalty. Feelings. What the fuck ever. Have them. I just want *you*. Pull my strings, every damned one of them. I was just trying to tell you what I thought you wanted to hear. Well actually," she paused, stood from the couch and walked to the far side of the living area.

She stared out the large window, "I was telling you I wouldn't feel emotion because that's what *most* guys want to hear. Hell, I didn't know what emotion was until you touched me."

"Now?" she turned and raised her hands to her head and scratched frantically.

Her hair fell down along her arms as she tossed it back and forth, "Now I feel like you've shoved your hand inside of me and are controlling my every move like I'm some fucking puppet. You hypnotize me when you talk to me Jak. The bad thing is this - I like it."

She released her hair and pushed her hands into the rear pockets of her jeans, "You're not going to fuck me over?"

I shook my head, "It'll never happen. And I'm not most guys."

KARTER

"I know you're not. And never? How can you say never?" she asked as she twisted her hips back and forth.

Standing in front of the window in what was probably her best pair of faded jeans, she looked adorable. The tee shirt she wore hugged her body like a glove, revealing a more athletic body than the loose fitting concert shirts she had worn previously. With her hands behind her and her shoulders high, her back arched. As she nervously twisted her body back and forth, I caught glimpses of the tattoos which covered her from upper bicep to the back of her hand.

"Karter," I paused and stood from the couch.

Positioned almost twenty feet from her, I was comfortable telling her how I felt. Any opposition from this distance would be easy for me to overcome. If she rejected me while I was holding her in my arms, I'd feel the pain for a lifetime.

"If you called me tomorrow and told me you couldn't see me for some reason, whatever that might be, I have no idea how I'd make it through the day. I'm fascinated by you. I think you're gorgeous. I want to kiss you, smell your hair, hold you in my arms, and touch every inch of your skin with my hands," I shook my head in sexual frustration as I studied her standing before me with her hands still pressed into the rear pockets of her jeans.

She twisted her hips back and forth and grinned. Overwhelmed by her simple beauty and my unwillingness to act upon my sexual desires, I shifted my gaze to my boots, "I want to see you naked. Hell, I want fuck you senseless, fall asleep with you in my arms and wake up and do it all over again. But that's not why I'm here Karter. It's not why I'm in your life or allowing you to be in mine. I'm here because you provide me with something I've never felt, and I don't know how I can live without *it* or without *you* for that matter. I really don't give an absolute fuck if I've known you a week or a year; you make me feel the way you make me feel. You and I *click,* Karter."

I realized I was fumbling with the change in my pockets and still staring at my boots. I felt like a little boy again. I had allowed myself to become human and went on a five minute rant about my feelings. She had said nothing in response. In hindsight, I really didn't give her an opportunity. Although I had so much more I felt I needed to say, I decided it was as good of a place as any to stop. I pulled my hands from my pockets and looked upward in hope of a verbal confirmation of feelings or rebuttal of some sort. Karter stood before me, shirtless. Her small but perky breasts were uncovered. On the floor beside her the tee shirt, shoes and bra she was wearing formed a small pile. She was barefoot, and making every effort to push the waist of her unbuttoned jeans down her thighs. She looked up as I studied her face. Her expression was one of playful wonder. It was as if she wanted confirmation what she was doing was acceptable. I smiled, reached down, and pulled my tee shirt over my head. I remained where I stood and bent down to unlace my boots while I continued to focus on her. As I unbuckled my belt and pressed my thumbs into the waist of my boxers, I paused. As she kicked her jeans from her feet, she reached for the waist of her panties. Quietly pulling her panties down her thighs, she smiled and winked one eye.

I hesitated and admired her tattoos as she fought to remove her underwear. Her entire shoulder and a portion of her upper chest were covered in a colorful floral display. As she lifted her foot from the floor and released them beside the pile of clothes, I pushed my boxers and jeans to the floor and kicked them aside.

"What the fuck!" she gasped.

KARTER

I suppose falling head over heels for someone and having them strip naked long after you're emotionally attached - only to reveal a cock the size of a peanut would be nothing short of horrific.

I stared at Jak's cock as I walked his direction.

I widened my eyes and shook my head, "Holy shit!"

"Do you slay dragons with that sword, Jak?"

"Say again?" he chimed.

"Nevermind," I said as I slowly walked his direction.

The closer I got, the larger it became. As I took the last step which separated us, I stared in awe of the size of his manhood. After a few repeated blinks, my eyes shifted upward and admired his torso. His body was not at all what I expected it to be. I knew all along he was in good physical shape, but his clothes hid all the good stuff. His stomach was flat and rippled with muscle. He had not a single ounce of fat on him anywhere. Although I had seen his thighs when he wore shorts, I had no idea his body was as chiseled and sculpted as it was. His upper arms bulged with muscles. From what I could see, he had only one tattoo on his left bicep - an eagle, anchor, pistol and pitchfork of some sort. His chest was wide and thick, and his waist small. Little *fuck me valleys* started at his lower abdomen and formed the shape of a 'V' as they stretched down toward his cock.

KARTER

I stared down at his half-stiff cock.

Houston, we have a problem.

The thought of him attempting to stuff it into my inexperienced pussy was equal parts scary and exciting. Although I told Jak I'd been with a handful of men, nothing could be further from the truth. My noncompliant pussy had prevented me from really ever *being* with anyone – sexually speaking. It wasn't that I hadn't tried, but frustration eventually set in with whoever I had attempted to have sex with and it always ended in a manner short of any form of satisfactory sexual romp. I was far from a virgin, but I was a comparable distance from being sexually *experienced*. One thing which separated Jak from any previous sexual attempts was the fact I was absolutely soaked.

"Is there a problem?" he asked softly as I wrapped my arms around his neck.

"No sir," I responded.

He reached down and slid his right hand behind my thighs and plucked me from the floor. As he nodded his head toward the two doors on the east wall, I smiled, "The left."

Something about being in Jak's arms made me feel like nothing mattered. It was as if I could spend the rest of my life needing nothing or no one else, as long as he'd pick me up from time to time. As I tried to come to some form of mental understanding of what had happened to my life in six short days, Jak lowered me to the bed. As his hands pressed into the comforter on either side of me, I pressed my elbows into the bed and raised my shoulders. As I made every effort to absorb what was happening, I stared at him admiringly. He carefully slid his hands to my stomach and began softly kissing my inner thighs. I closed my eyes. Watching his naked body was far more than I was prepared for.

He kissed along my thighs, up to my hips, and rested his mouth on my stomach. As he kissed along my torso, his hands slid to my chest. His fingers gently touched my nipples as his mouth worked its way to my neck. I moaned as his teeth nibbled against my collar bone. As his lips encompassed the bottom of my ear, a chill ran from my neck to my toes.

Waiting for Jak to move from foreplay to sex was so much more than difficult. I enjoyed his mouth against my skin and his lips softly kissing my neck, but I yearned for him to take the next step. In my mind, I longed for the commitment that came along with sex. It wasn't that I necessarily wanted the act of sex, but I deeply desired everything I expected to come with it. Right or wrong, I felt I understood enough about Jak to know if he mentally committed to have sex with me, he would remain invested – at least until I fucked something up – and I had no intention of fucking anything up. I believed if he had sex with me, this thing between us could - and should - last forever.

I desperately wanted forever with Jak.

I felt his hand between my legs. The tip of his finger began to massage my clit softly. I licked my lips and attempted to focus on the feeling building in the pit of my stomach. As his finger slid down from my clit against my wet pussy, I moaned.

He paused.

No, keep going.

"I like it," I sighed.

His finger worked in and out of my wetness as his lips kissed and sucked my nipples. I felt tremendous pressure building inside of me. I felt guilty, strange, weird, and wonderful all at the same time. I bit my lip. Slowly and predictably, his finger slid in and out of me. I opened my eyes as I felt a huge mental and physical release.

Holy fuck.

That's what I'm talking about. That shit right there.

I pressed my arms into the mattress and raised my upper back from the comforter. I opened my eyes and caught my breath, "I want you inside of me, Jak."

He looked up and into my eyes. Without speaking, his mouth kissed up my neck and to my lips. I closed my eyes. After several long passionate kisses, I was emotionally on fire. Kissing had never been anything which interested me, but now? Holy fuck I liked being kissed by Jak. He bit my lower lip lightly and licked the tip of my tongue as our mouths parted. Our mouths met again and he pressed his lips hard against mine. I flicked my tongue against his, knowing nothing of what I should do; only attempting to repeat what he had been doing. I liked this, and I liked it a lot. As our lips parted, I opened my eyes. He touched my face with his hand, and sparks shot throughout my entire body. The touch of his hands alone was enough. Without a doubt, to me, Jak was magical. I stared past his gorgeous looks and into his eyes.

Please don't dick me over. I think I've already fallen in love with you.

"If we do this, you have to keep me. Okay?" I breathed.

"I'm keeping you either way," he whispered.

I bit my lower lip and nodded my head slightly.

I spread my legs as wide as I was able. Jak nestled between my thighs and softly pressed himself against me. As the tip of his cock pressed against my wet pussy, I bit my lip harder and opened my eyes slightly. Softly, he began to kiss my chin. As I felt him begin to slide inside of me, I opened my mouth. As he continued to slide inside, I arched my back slightly and gasped. His eyes widened.

I batted my eyes and attempted to smile. I felt like weeping. Not bad tears, but a form of crying I was not aware even existed. My mind ached to scream, and my eyes yearned to water. I felt as if the tips of thousand knives were poking me gently. Slowly and softly, he worked himself in and out of my swollen wetness. I pressed my hands into his chest and gripped his skin with my fingertips. I felt connected to Jak, and not through sex, it was much more than that.

As he slowly worked himself in and out, his hands caressed every inch of my body. Without any concept of time or an idea of when we started or how long it had lasted, my feelings of euphoria began to mount. As he pressed his mouth to mine, our tongues fought for ownership of the space we shared. Pressure built within me.

I screamed into his mouth.

My everything exploded.

And in my mind, Jak and I became fused together.

I had never been one to believe in love, fairy tales, or happily ever after horseshit like every other girl in school. I believed it was possible for a man and a woman to meet, end up having sex, and stay together until they grew apart. Infrequently a couple might stay together until they died, but for me to try and believe they were faithful for that timeframe was impossible. When people told me they were in love, mentally I rolled my eyes and said *give it time*.

I truly believed and totally accepted I would live my life alone, painting abstract art no one would ever understand but me. I could never paint fast enough to eliminate all of the thoughts which collected in my head. My mind a jumbled mess of colors, shapes, and phrases, I raced from canvas to canvas to attempt to rid myself of the fog between my ears for even a moment; but the moment never came.

My mind was a perpetual whirlwind of everything and nothing. My only fleeting moments of sanity came infrequently from either riding my bike or slinging paint onto a canvas.

Until now.

We had laid silently for an immeasurable amount of time. I opened my eyes and moaned. His hands pressed into the comforter beside me, and his chest lifted from mine, he slowly smiled his dimple smile and began to speak.

"I…uhhm," his voice faultered.

He paused, closed his eyes, and shook his head.

My mind, for the first time I had ever known, was empty short of one thought and one feeling. Jak opened his eyes. I extended my index finger and moved my hand between our faces.

I love this man. I know it.

"I think I love you," I blurted.

"I'm one step ahead of ya, Karter," he breathed as he pushed my hand to the side and kissed me.

"How so?" I asked as he softly released my lips from his.

"I *know* I love you," he sighed.

My eyes welled with tears.

Awwwe. Fuck.

I squirmed and attempted to sit up slightly. I swallowed heavily, "No matter what happens, no matter what dumb shit I do - and just know I'll do something - please tell me we can work through it. Don't ever just leave me, okay? Give me a chance to fix it."

"Don't cheat on me Karter. Ever. And we'll be fine," he smiled.

"It'll never happen," I promised.

"Never is a long time, Karter," he said softly.

I pushed my hands against his chest and attempted to shove him away, "Seriously, Jak? I don't have a choice, because as far as I'm concerned, there's only one man on this earth, and that man is you."

"Fair enough," he laughed.

"You dork," I responded.

I rolled my eyes and sighed. Jak was gorgeous, handsome, sincere, tough and cute. What more would any woman want?

As we relaxed on the top of the comforter naked, the air conditioning system cycled on. We both turned and looked at each other. The cold air blowing against my naked body felt freezing. I pulled the pillows from the head of the bed and yanked back the comforter. Simultaneously, we both crawled into the bed. Mentally and physically exhausted, I rolled onto my side and clutched my pillow as Jak pressed his naked body against mine. As I filled myself with thoughts of Jak and me making love, I fell asleep in his arms.

I woke up and looked around the dimly lit room. Jak lay beside me asleep. I desperately needed to pee. Quietly, I slipped my feet from under the comforter and onto the floor. I walked to the bathroom and peed. As I meandered to the kitchen and got a drink of water, I attempted to recall all of the events from the last twenty-four hours.

Still naked, I walked to the window and looked outside. The parking lot was empty. I looked at the screen of my computer. It was 3:20 a.m. I stood quietly and listened. I could hear Jak's faint snoring from the bedroom. Quietly, I logged onto the computer and opened Google. I typed four words into the text box.

Eagle, anchor, pitchfork, and pistol.

I pressed enter.

The first site to pop up was Wikipedia. I didn't need to go to any others. Jak's exact tattoo was on their website.

Special Warfare?

Navy SEAL?

The tattoo was called a SEAL Trident.

Jak wasn't a badass.

Jak was the baddest of all bad asses.

Holy shit.

For over an hour I read everything I could about Navy SEALS. It explained a lot. Jak would never fuck me over. Jak was in it for the long haul. Jak would protect me from harm. I went to a military records website and typed in Jak's name and branch of service.

Jak Anderson Kennedy. U.S.N., retired.

D.O.B. 8 Jan 1976.

Jak was thirty-eight years old. I could care less how old he was. As long as he didn't find out my age right away, we should be just fine. Eventually I knew I'd have to tell him, but for now? If he didn't ask me, I would keep it my little secret. The thought of losing Jak over a little difference in age seemed quite stupid the more I thought of it. I cleared my history from the internet, logged off the computer and walked back to the bedroom.

Quietly, I crawled into bed with a man I obviously knew very little about.

But loved with all my heart.

JAK

She closed one eye as she blew a cloud of smoke from her lungs. In what had become a more health conscious world with far less people smoking, my mother continued to chain smoke cigarettes in her home as if she had no knowledge of them being detrimental to her health. As the last of the smoke cleared her lips, she looked down at her hand as if confused, "What's her name again?"

"Karter, mom. Her name is Karter, spelled with a 'K'," I said as I raised my coffee cup to my lips.

"I thought you said Martha. It's a good thing I asked, Jak," she said as she pressed her cigarette into the overstuffed ashtray.

I chuckled and shook my head lightly, "Shhh. She's going to hear you."

She widened her eyes and stared across the table, "It sounded like you said Martha. I can't help it you mumble. I hear just fine."

"Mom, you need a hearing aid. I'll pay for it. And you're going to burn the house down if you keep smoking in here. No one smokes anymore. We should get you an e-cigarette, they're healthy," I smiled.

She scrunched her brow and tapped the cigarette case lying on the table beside her coffee cup, "I like *real* cigarettes. I don't want to smoke battery powered smoke sticks, Jak."

She picked up her coffee cup and raised it half the distance to her mouth, "She's beautiful, Jak. How tall is she? And she has more tattoos than you do," she sighed.

She lowered her coffee cup and leaned into the edge of the table. Her eyes shifted side-to-side and she attempted her best to whisper, "She has them on her hands, Jak."

"Mom, stop. I know she does. On one hand, and I like them. She's an artist, a painter. She's good for me, she really is."

"I know she is Jak. I can see it, I'm your mother, remember. I raised you. I know what's good for you. I like her. She's pretty and I like her hair," she said as she leaned into the back of her chair.

My mother was a saint. She was the type of person to potentially question a person's preferences to herself, but not outwardly. She was never critical of even the worst people. In her eyes, God created everyone equal, and they remained so regardless of the choices they made in life. Even the worst criminals weren't necessarily bad people in my mother's eyes, they only made poor decisions.

I didn't offer Karter's age, and my mother didn't ask. It wouldn't matter to her one way or another, but I felt no real need to mention it; at least not at this point in time. I wasn't certain if Karter realized she revealed her age when we were in the Mediterranean restaurant, but I certainly noticed whether she knew it or not. To me, it didn't matter. Karter provided me with an inner comfort unlike anything I had ever imagined was even possible. We are incapable of forcing ourselves to fall in love with someone we are not attracted to, and certainly less able of preventing a love which is predestined to be.

"Mom? Do you believe in destiny?" I asked.

She shook her head and pulled a cigarette from her case. As she lit it, she closed one eye and shook her head from side to side, "God has a plan for each and every one of us, Jak. Look at your father."

She paused and blew the smoke at her feet. As she looked up, she shook her head again and snuffed the fresh cigarette into the ashtray, "It was destiny. God's will. Destiny *is* God's will. Are you asking me about the girl?"

I nodded my head once and turned to face the hallway as I heard the bathroom door open. As Karter walked down the hallway toward the kitchen, I felt somewhat foolish for asking a question I already knew the answer to. My mother truly believed everything happened in God's world for a reason.

Everything.

She stood from her seat and picked up her coffee cup, "If she makes you feel the way you say she does, it can't be anything but destiny, Jak. God broke her motorcycle for a reason."

"Are you okay, honey?" my mother asked as Karter stepped into the kitchen.

"Yes ma'am. My stomach is a little queasy, that's all," Karter smiled.

"Stand up and pull her chair out, Jak. You weren't born in a barn," my mother sighed over her shoulder.

I turned toward Karter and rolled my eyes as I stood. As I pulled her chair from the table she sat and smiled. Simply seeing her smile provided me with a level of satisfaction I hoped I would one day experience, but had no expectation of it ever coming to be. In being honest with myself and realizing this peace of mind hinged on Karter's presence, I came to truly understand I was incapable of living a fulfilling life without her. We had known each other all of three weeks. Be that it as it may, it did not change how having Karter share her life with me caused me to feel. As Karter reached for her cup of coffee, I admired her freshly painted fingernails.

"Honey, hand Jak your cold coffee. Jak, bring me that cup and I'll get her a new one. Cold coffee will upset her stomach," my mother said without looking up, her face obstructed by the refrigerator door.

Karter turned to me and smiled as she slid the coffee cup in front of me. I knew better than to argue with my mother. I stood and carried the coffee cup to the sink. After dumping the out the luke-warm coffee, I poured a fresh cup and turned toward the table.

"Slow down, Jak. Take her this, it'll make her stomach feel better," my mother whispered as she handed me a small plate of sliced cheese.

My mother found all of life's questions answered by a slice of cheese. When she was upset, she ate cheese. When she wanted a snack, she ate cheese. When she was happy, she ate cheese. She covered her left overs with cheese, and then believed she was eating different food altogether. As a child, many of my stomach aches were resolved - according to my mother - by the cheese she force fed me. My mother was not a selfish woman – in fact she was quite the opposite. But to my mother, her cheese was sacred. Seeing her offer it to Karter as a form of remedy to her upset stomach allowed me to understand my mother had truly accepted Karter as being a permanent part of my life; and hers.

"Honey, nibble on that cheese, it'll make you feel better," my mother said as she poured herself a fresh cup of coffee.

"Karter, did you grow up around here?" my mother asked.

Before I could attempt to change the subject, Karter responded. I had purposely not asked Karter of her upbringing nor did she offer. As a result, she never asked specifically of my childhood or where I went to school. The majority of what we had *not* discussed was a result of me not necessarily being completely satisfied with our age variance being a non-issue. It made no difference to me, but I feared the seventeen years which separated us may make a difference to her. If asked, I would be truthful. If not, I had no intention of simply offering my age. Her open admission of her age, by mistake or not, made me fractionally less comfortable allowing her find out mine. Without a doubt, in time, there would be no secrets between us.

"I grew up in Hartford." Karter smiled over her shoulder.

"Connecticut?" my mother smiled as she sat down.

"Yes ma'am, Connecticut."

"Brothers? Sisters?" my mother asked as she sipped her coffee.

"No ma'am. I'm an only child. And both my parents are deceased," Karter responded flatly.

My heart immediately sank for Karter. Instinctively, I wanted to know more. I knew not to ask. Some things are best left unasked and unanswered. Commander Warrenson's words came to mind as I sat and waited for my mother to respond.

Never turn over a rock if you aren't prepared to discuss what may lie beneath it.

"I'm sorry to hear that. Well, Wichita is a fine city. For as big as it is, it's also as small as you'll let it be. You can come see me anytime; you don't need to bring Jak with you, honey. Give her my phone number Jak," my mother sighed.

She turned toward Karter and inventoried her from head to toe, "How tall are you, honey?"

Her eyes focused on me, Karter narrowed her gaze and turned toward my mother, "Excuse me?"

"How tall are you, honey? You seem tall for a girl."

"Mom, everyone is tall to you. You're five feet nothing," I laughed.

KARTER

My mother lowered her coffee cup and scowled my direction. Karter alternated glances between my mother and I, and eventually became fixed on my mother.

"Five-six."

"You're six foot if you're an inch," my mother argued.

My mother pointed to what she called the *junk drawer*, "Get the tape measure out of the drawer. Let's measure her, Jak."

"Mom…"

"It's fine, Jak," Karter said as she stood from her chair.

As if it was a common occurrence, Karter stood and walked to the doorway which led to the living room. As she backed up to the wooden trim, she straightened her posture and stood arrow straight, smiling. I shook my head in disbelief and opened the drawer behind me. I removed the tape measure and extended the end to the floor. As I raised my arm over Karter's head, tape measure in hand, my mother stood. I watched as she opened a drawer behind her and eventually walked our direction.

"Here. Hold her hair flat with this butter knife, so you get it right, Jak," she said as she shook a butter knife in front of me.

I looked down at the knife, and up into my mother's eyes. I tossed my head toward the table and furrowed my brow. I turned toward Karter, and stared at the rule behind her head. As I studied the inch declaration on the face of the rule, my mother reached around me and pushed down on Karter's hair with the blade of the butter knife. Karter rolled her eyes and smiled.

"Well, I don't have my glasses, what does it say?" My mother asked.

"Five foot six, on the money," I responded.

Karter thrust her hands into the air as if she had won the lottery, "Told ya."

"You're six foot if you're an inch, honey. There's something wrong with that damned thing. Always has been," my mother hissed as she lowered the butter knife and turned to the kitchen.

As I retracted the steel tape measure into the case, Karter stood with her back against the wooden door trim. She looked into my eyes and smiled. Her eyes were a translucent green, and a complete compliment to her skin and hair color. As I continued to admire her, I became lost momentarily - simply standing in front of her and staring. She leaned into me and after a soft hesitation of uncertainty, kissed me softly on the lips.

Karter's carefree attitude, fearless nature, and expressed love for me allowed me to accept life as being without fault. With her in my life, I had no room for anything else to creep in. In her absence, without a doubt, my life would be nothing but turmoil. Karter filled me so full of what was good, that the bad I had spent two decades witnessing never had an opportunity to come to the surface. Karter was not only filling my heart with love, she was undoubtedly saving me from myself.

"See," my mother said.

I turned her direction as she paused.

"She couldn't kiss you like that if she wasn't six feet tall, Jak."

At that moment I realized to my mother, not unlike me, Karter was as big as life itself. I turned my head and smiled over my left shoulder, "You're right, mom. There's something wrong with that thing."

I turned to face Karter and puckered my lips. As I slowly moved my mouth to hers, I winked my left eye, "Always has been."

JAK

"Well, if a man looks in the scripture, there's no reference to it. They took the time to make a statement about all other things a man can imagine. Stand to reason Jak, if there was somethin' wrong with it in the Lord's eyes, he'd a made sure and got it writ down in there somewhere. As a matter of fact," Oscar paused and rubbed his goatee.

He nodded his head and smiled, "Sarah was ten years younger'n Abraham."

"I'm talking a few more years than that," I sighed.

"Don't think it matters, Jak. You tryin' to talk yourself out of it?" he asked as he pulled a cigar from his pocket.

"No sir. Just two men talking, that's all. There are only three people I trust right now, Oscar - you, her, and my mother. And neither of them have any concern about age differences. I'm just asking you man to man, that's all."

"Well I'll give you my opinion about it, 'cause I know that's what you come for. You see, life is about quality, not quantity. You know that, right?" he asked as he raised the cigar to his lips.

I nodded my head, not quite sure what he meant; but confident he'd expand upon the point he was trying to make sooner or later.

He pulled the cigar from his mouth and pointed the tip of it toward me, "Let's see. Say a man is married for fifty years. Say he met his wife in high school. Maybe they was sweethearts. Got married at say, oh hell, eighteen years of age. Now they's sixty-eight, Jak. And they lived a life of drunkenness by him; and let's say he's mean as a damned snake when he drinks. And he's a cheatin' on her and comin' home drunk and slappin' her around for fifty solid years. That ain't a very good fifty years of marriage, now is it?"

"No sir," I responded.

"And if someone like you meets someone like Karter, and they have the same age difference, but let's say they ain't you - for sayin's sake. If they's as happy as you two seem to be, and let's say they live twenty years together. And every day, Jak," he paused and shook his cigar.

"Every damned one was as good as the last. And they's a runnin' and a playin' and having fun, and livin' life to the fullest. Hell, they can't imagine livin' without each other. These two ain't a fightin' or a fussin'. Not even once. They's meant to be in the eyes of all who see 'em, and in God's eyes too. So, God bless her soul, the lady gets cancer and she dies, Jak. After twenty years. Now would that twenty year relationship be better'n that fifty year one where the man was a drunken snake?" he raised his cigar to his lips and bit on the plastic tip.

"I suppose it would, yes," I smiled and nodded.

"Quality, Jak. Not quantity. That's gonna be today's lesson. I like that," he said through his teeth.

"I like it too, thanks Oscar."

"I ain't done yet," he growled lightly.

I shrugged, "What else you got, old man?"

He shook his head and pulled the cigar from his mouth, "Love Jak. A man once told me love was blind. You know what? He was damned sure right. Love don't see a damned thing. Not *real* love. It don't see color, or religion, neighborhoods, poverty or wealth. Hell, it don't even see age differences for that matter. Real love just snaps into place. You ever had that black old heart of yours broke, Jak?"

I considered his question. I had, but felt no need to discuss details. A simple *yes* should suffice.

"Yes sir," I responded.

He turned to the workbench and picked up his coffee cup. As he turned around, he smiled. Slowly, he walked in front of me with the cup held at his side. When he was about ten feet in front of me, he stopped and lifted the cup to his chest. As he raised one eyebrow and opened his eyes in a comical fashion, he dropped it on the concrete floor. The porcelain cup shattered in countless pieces on the floor. Shocked, I looked up. Oscar smiled.

"Now if I give you that pile of busted shit off the floor and a tube of glue out of my cabinet, you thinkin' you can fix it where I'd never know it was broke?"

I shook my head and laughed, "No sir."

"You consider yourself pretty able, don't ya?" he asked as he began to scoop the pieces into a pile with his boot.

I smiled and nodded my head, "Yes sir."

"Well, as able as you are, you couldn't fix this sum bitch no how. You might get it put back together best you could, and it'd look like a cup; but there's gonna be some pieces you can't find, and there's gonna be some others just don't make good sense. You know the ones you look at in about eleventeen different directions and they just look like they belong to a different cup," he looked up from the floor and raised the cigar to his lips.

"You see my point?" he asked.

KARTER

"Yes sir," I smiled.

"Well, that cup's your heart, Jak. That's what happens when someone busts you up good inside. You end up with a bunch of pieces you did your best with, and they make a heart, but it ain't quite right. That fucker'd leak coffee on your trousers if you tried to fill her up. Now, to fix it, and it can be fixed; it sure can," he paused and reached into his pocket.

He pulled out his lighter and lit the cigar. After a few short puffs, he blew a cloud of sweet smoke into the air and grinned, "You need one of them filler glues. The ones that go into each and every crack and crevice. That shit fills holes you can't even see."

He puffed on the cigar and blew another cloud of smoke in the air.

"Love Jak. Love is the filler glue. It's why when you love someone, nothin' else matters. Because the woman you're in love with fills all of the broken parts inside of you, even the ones you don't see."

He shook his cigar at my face as he spoke, "When you *think* you love someone, and you ain't sure, you got nothin' more than a leaky old cup. That's why you question the love. Because you got some pieces missin' and some leaky holes. Me? I'm thinkin' little ole Miss Karter's done filled your holes right up. She's filled your old busted heart with love, an' you ain't leakin' anymore."

I smiled and looked down at the broken cup. Oscar had an odd way of making his point, but he seemed to do so in a manner I would always be able to remember.

Oscar tapped the tip of the cigar against his lip and closed his eyes. At this point, I knew him well enough to know he was thinking about something, and he wasn't quite done talking. As he opened his eyes, he puffed his cigar.

"Let me ask you a question, Jak. I know ain't none of us lookin' to get in a discussion about it, but I'll make it's as easy as a yes or no. You thought about the war since you an' Miss Karter got together? You remembered any of the faces of them men ya killed, Jak?"

The three days before I met Karter were filled with doubt, regret, and feelings of worthlessness. I felt depressed and alone. Since meeting her, I had not thought about the war one single time. My thoughts, and my *only* thoughts, had been about her or our potential future together. Thoughts and feelings of her had filled me to the point there was no room for anything else.

"Haven't thought about it once," I responded.

He turned to face his work bench and blew a cloud of smoke into the air, "Go climb that tree Jak."

"Thanks Oscar. I'll be seeing you."

Not if I see you first.

"Not if I see you first," he laughed.

KARTER

"This is it?" I laughed as I motioned around the sparsely furnished apartment.

Jak's apartment looked like someone was either almost moved out or thinking about beginning to move in. One small couch, a chair, and a wooden trunk which was used for an end table were the extent of the furnishings in the apartment. I slowly spun in a circle and scanned from floor to the high ceilings. Not one picture, photograph, painting, or piece of art hung on the walls. Jak stood half the distance between the door and the carpeted living area and watched me. I walked to the bedroom door and peered inside. A queen size bed with a plain white comforter was pressed against the center of the far wall. White pillows cases covered two pillows. A five drawer chest was positioned perfectly between the bed and the wall.

Two on the couch, and one in the chair, that's it. Three people, not including the bedroom.

"Are you going to bring in more stuff?" I asked as I turned from the bedroom.

"I hadn't planned on it," he shrugged.

"You don't even have a table or chairs. There's no art, no decorative flair, no plants, no lamps, no real sign of life, and no," I paused as shook my head.

KARTER

"It's empty. You have an empty apartment," I laughed.

"I have all I need right here," he smiled as he motioned around the apartment.

"I beg to differ," I said as I rolled my eyes.

My apartment looked like an eclectic collection of junk. It was no different than my mind – cluttered. I had too much furniture, far too many pieces of art, too much decorative bullshit, and too little room. Being in Jak's apartment reminded me of a hospital room. Only the barest of necessities existed. For Jak and Jak's way of living for the last twenty years, I'm sure he felt it was enough. Jak still hadn't offered to tell me what his occupation was, and although I knew, I had yet to ask him. I figured in time he'd tell me, but so far he hadn't. In the last month with Jak, I had become more comfortable with him knowing my age. Part of me hesitated to tell him for fear of not knowing what his response may be. Another part of me wanted to tell him and get it over with. I decided to do two things; make a donation to Jak's empty apartment and go fishing for answers.

"So, I'm thinking I want to paint you a picture. What are your favorite colors?" I asked as I walked his direction.

"On a painting? I'd say reds and purples. Maybe yellow," he smiled.

I pointed at the far wall. It was roughly thirty feet in length, probably sixteen feet tall and free of any form of decoration, "Okay, I'm going to paint you a picture of me. A huge fucker - that way even if we aren't together, you can have me with you every night. What do you think of that?"

"I like it," he grinned.

Okay, one down one to go.

I smiled and took a slow absorbing look over the empty apartment for effect.

How can you live like this?

Do you like living like this?

How long have you lived like this?

"How long have you lived like this?" I asked.

"I've been here roughly a month," he responded.

I should have guessed he'd give evasive answers and provide nothing of substance. His super-secret SEAL training probably prevented him from naturally offering anything. But he wasn't talking to a novice. I could squeeze blood from a turnip.

"So have you always lived like this?" I sighed as I waved my arm in a circle.

He nodded his head, "Yes, as a matter of fact I have."

Jesus Jak. Seriously?

I scrunched my nose and shook my head lightly, "What allows a man to live like this?"

He shrugged his shoulders, "Men are different than women. I've learned to be satisfied with far less than most."

Learned to?

Okay...

"How'd you *learn* to, Jak? How does one learn to enjoy or be satisfied with less?"

He looked around the apartment as if satisfied, "Over time, I suppose. I've lived like this for my entire adult life."

I mentally rolled my eyes. Trying to force Jak to talk about something he wasn't willing or ready to discuss would be impossible. Hell, from what I had read on the internet, he was trained to withhold information even if he was tortured by terrorists. My simple questions weren't going to trick him into offering something he guarded as a secret. I decided a simpler more direct route may work to my benefit.

"What do you think could pull us apart?" I asked.

"Pull us apart? End our relationship?" he asked.

I nodded my head and turned toward the couch. As I walked away from him, he followed close behind.

"I don't know. Why would you ask such a thing?" he asked as he sat down on the end of the couch.

"Just wondering," I responded as I sat down beside him.

"Infidelity I suppose. To be completely honest, I don't know if I could make it through you cheating on me. I'd say that's it. Same question to you?" he said as he leaned against the arm of the couch.

"If you cheated on me I might leave you. I'm not giving you a free pass, but I'd probably eventually get over it if you fucked someone else. I can't say for sure if I'd leave you or not. Truthfully Jak, I really can't imagine ever being without you. The more I'm with you, the more I realize being without you isn't really an option. Well, *that* and I like fucking you," I smiled.

He rolled his eyes and grinned, revealing his dimples.

"So if I told you some crazy deep dark secret or revealed something about me you didn't know, you don't think it's possible you'd freak out and say *damn, I never would have guessed that,* and decide it's just too much? You know? And leave?" I shrugged.

The more I talked, the more I wanted to be totally honest and reveal my age. I didn't want to take the risk if I wasn't comfortable, and I preferred Jak say something to make me comfortable. I was ready to rid myself of all the secrets between us and continue a life together without wonder. Well, almost all the secrets, anyway.

He shook his head, "Not a chance."

"None whatsoever?" I asked.

"Nope," he smiled.

I stared into my lap, "I'm twenty-one years old, Jak."

"I know," he responded.

You know?

You cocksucker. What did you do? Investigate me? Pull some SEAL background investigation on me? And you don't care? You love me anyway? Get undressed Jak, let's celebrate with sex.

I turned to face him, "You knew?"

He nodded his head and smiled a soft smile, "Right after we met, we were eating in the place on Rock. *Adrian's*. It was the day the guy about hit you on your bike. You said your age."

I crossed my arms and exhaled loudly, "I most certainly did not."

Jak looked down at the floor for a moment, shifted his gaze to meet mine, and smiled his shitty little smirk, "I can't make it dry. Not around you. Nope. Just less wet. So Jak, now I'm *twenty-one years old* and I've had my first wet pussy. You want to secure a place in my heart? Alrighty then. You can check that box. You did that a long time ago."

Holy shit, he's right. And he's obviously going to remember every word I ever say. Note to self - be careful what you tell Jak.

"I guess I did," I sighed.

I raised my eyebrows and half-smiled, "You don't care?"

He bit his lip and shook his head from side-to-side, "Not in the least."

Well, if he knows I'm twenty-one, and he doesn't care, we're going to be just fine. I know his age and I don't give a fuck. He knows his age and he doesn't give a fuck. All that's left is him becoming comfortable with me knowing his age.

"How old are you, Jak?"

Shit. I wish I hadn't...

"Thirty-eight," he responded flatly.

He crossed his arms in front of his chest, "I'm thirty-eight, and I just retired from the Navy after a little more than twenty years. I have no idea what I'm going to do with the rest of my life as far as a career goes, but for now I'm satisfied doing what I'm doing. I don't *need* to work, but I feel I should."

"You were sailor?" I asked.

That should get him riled up, calling him a simple sailor.

He nodded his head sharply.

Damn, Jak. Modest much?

I turned my body to face him and pushed my feet under his thighs, "Well, I wouldn't care if you were twenty-one or fifty-one. I'm in love with you, and not because I chose to be. It's like the moment I met you, someone flipped a switch and changed everything within me. It just happened. I'd call it destiny, but really? There's no such thing. I know when we're together, my mind feels at ease. I've spent my entire life frantic, and I didn't know why. I think I was looking, searching…"

"For?" he asked.

I pushed my feet further under his thigh, "You, I guess. I think I've spent my life frantically searching for you."

"You ever want to get married?" he asked.

Do I ever want to get married?

My mind raced. I would marry Jak in a minute. His question was more rhetoric than anything. He was asking if I *believed* in marriage. If it was something I'd consider in the future. Marriage, to me, was nothing more than a piece of paper. But I'd be lying if I didn't admit I'd love to be married to Jak someday. The thought filled me with warmth.

"I'd love to be married someday," I responded proudly.

Jak looked down into his lap as if embarrassed, "I was married seventeen years ago. For about six months. I was deployed and when I came home she was with another man. I filed for divorce and haven't been with anyone since."

I sat up in my seat and smiled, "Not a single relationship? Seventeen years?"

"Not an *anything*. I haven't been with a woman from the day I walked out until now. Not one," he shook his head and sighed.

"Not at all? No blowjobs in Japan or Asian fuck swings in Taiwan?" I laughed.

"No. I've been celibate, only masturbation," he chuckled as he stroked his hand over his crotch jokingly.

No sex? Holy shit. And after seventeen years, he picked me?

Immediately I felt privileged and extremely comfortable with Jak and I being a couple. It wasn't so much an uncomfortable feeling I felt before, but now I felt as if together we could conquer the world. Over the last month, sex with Jak had become more comfortable for me. Each time we had sex, I became a little more adventurous and less like a little girl who was falling deeper into some fairly tale version of love. Fucking Jak was the icing on the cake of our relationship.

"I have a short term and a long term request," I smiled as I pulled my feet from under his thigh.

He grinned and nodded once, "Let's hear it."

I scooted across the small couch and wrapped my arms around his neck, "Long term? One day I want to be your wife."

He smiled and kissed my lips lightly, "Great. I want that as well."

KARTER

"Short term? This place creeps me out. Let's walk over to my loft and fuck. I like it when you fuck me," I batted my eyes and waited for a response.

"I like fucking you," he smiled.

"Okay, let's go. I'm ready," I stood from the couch and grinned, "hopefully your old ass won't have a heart attack on the way over there."

He stood from the couch and raised one eyebrow, "Say again? Did you call me old?"

I looked down at his boots smiled. I glanced at my Chuck's. There was no way he could outrun me in boots. No way. I needed to make a quick exit. I glanced toward the door and made sure I had a clear shot.

"They say the hearing is the first sign of old age," I paused and grinned.

I cupped my hands around my mouth and screamed, "Hopefully your old ass won't have a heart attack on the way over there."

And I took off in a dead run toward the door. Hopefully when he caught me, if he caught me, he'd grudge fuck me and teach me a lesson about respect.

A girl can always reserve hope.

KARTER

As the elevator doors began to close, I heard his boots on the floor of the hallway. With twelve inches of space left between the closing doors, I watched Jak come around the corner. I continued to press the *close* button with my thumb as I waved with my free hand and smiled. Relieved to have won the race, I sighed as the elevator began to rise. He was able to run much faster in his boots than I ever would have imagined. Luckily, I caught a break in cross traffic and ran between two oncoming cars. Jak had to wait for another pause in traffic before he was able to cross the street. The sixty second head start wasn't enough to overcome his strength, stamina, and determination to catch me. The closer we got to my five story building, the less distance separated us. At least now I would be able to lock him out of my apartment until he cooled off.

Then he could grudge fuck me.

I stood in the elevator and waited for it to reach the fifth floor. I was out of breath and obviously a little more out of shape than I had thought. As the elevator dinged and the doors opened, I sighed and attempted to catch my breath. The old elevator would have to go back to the first floor and pick up Jak, so I should have plenty of time. As I walked the length of the hallway to my loft, I smiled at the thought of Jak fucking me. Everything about him excited me, but when we made love it was almost unexplainable.

I reached into my pocket and fought to find my keys as I turned the corner toward my doorway. As I looked up, Jak was leaning on the door, smiling.

He raised one eyebrow, "Old ass? Heart attack?"

I'm fucked.

He wasn't even short of breath. I blinked my eyes and stared. *What the fuck?* There was only one elevator. Navy SEAL or not, impossible was impossible, and *this* was impossible. I pulled the keys from the pocket of my shorts and reached for the lock. Jak continued to glare at me with the stink eye.

"How..."

Jak nodded his head toward the stairs, "Stairs."

"You ran up five flights of stairs? Before I..." I shook my head in disbelief and didn't even finish my sentence.

He nodded his head.

"Are you going to teach me a..."

"Lesson?" he asked before I finished speaking.

I lowered my head in disgrace. Something about playing a trick on Jak didn't seem quite so funny now. I pushed the key into the lock and opened the door. As the door opened, Jak motioned inside and grinned.

Well, at least he's not mad.

"Get your little ass in there," he demanded as he waved his arm in the opening.

Maybe he is mad. I wonder what he's going to...

He pointed to the corner and spoke in a stern voice, "Get over by the canvas you're working on and strip down to nothing. Stand on the right side of the easel naked and don't move."

This is the punishment? I'll call you old and feeble every day.

Eagerly, I pranced to the easel and pulled off my shoes and socks. After removing my shorts and panties, I realized Jak hadn't removed anything. Wondering just what he had planned, I removed my shirt and fumbled to remove my bra.

"What are you going to..."

"Naked, Karter. Get the bra off," he demanded as he stood in front of me with his hands on his hips.

I did my best to salute him, "Yes sir."

He rolled his eyes and pointed to my chest, "Bra. Take it off."

As I tossed my bra to the floor, he walked between the easel and where I stood. He turned to face the canvas I had been working on, and admired it for a moment, "Do you have the canvas you were going to start painting on for me? The one you mentioned *before* you called me old?"

"It's against the wall, behind you," I responded softly.

Fully dressed, Jak walked to the wall and pulled the blank from the floor. Standing naked, I felt awkward with Jak fully clothed. I wondered what he was going to do to me. I tried to imagine what might be next, but based on my lack of experience of being in trouble with Jak, I drew a complete blank. I didn't want to think for one minute about causing Jak to feel old or incapable, because he was far from either. To think of him being disappointed in me caused me to feel uneasy. I wanted to make Jak happy and keep him that way. As he walked toward the easel with the canvas, he turned to me and smiled.

"Stamina, Karter. I have it. Additionally, I'm head strong. I, however, have my doubts about you. Here's what we're going to do. You're going to start painting - naked. More specifically, you're going to start painting the picture you spoke of earlier. At no point in time are you going to stop painting and study me or stare at me, do you understand?" he asked in a very matter-of-fact tone.

Somewhat confused, I nodded my head, "Yes sir. What are you going to do?"

"Well, now that you've asked, I suppose I'll tell you. I'm going to stand here and stroke my cock. And I'm not going to stop until I cum. You're not allowed to speak or stare, only take an occasional glance," he responded without so much as cracking a smile.

This is punishment?

He removed my painting from the easel and replaced it with the new canvas. He knelt down and untied his boots. After removing the boots and socks, he unbuckled his jeans and tossed them aside. After pulling his tee shirt over his head, he stood and began rubbing his cock through his boxer shorts. Almost instantly, his rigid cock stretched his boxers beyond their design limit. As he leaned down and removed my palette from the floor and gathered some tubes of paint, I felt myself getting wet. I swallowed heavily. There had to be more to it than this. I pressed my knees together and winced as I realized the extent of my wetness. I had questions I felt I needed to ask before we got started.

With his broad back facing me and standing in his boxer shorts, he squeezed various colors of paint onto the palette. His bicep muscles flexed as he twisted the lids on the tubes and tossed them onto the drop cloth on the floor beside the easel. It was sheer torture watching him stand half-naked as he prepared for the sexual escapades he had described.

"Can I touch myself?" I asked.

"Absolutely not. At least I better not catch you doing it," he snapped.

Oh God. This is going to be so hot.

"What are we going to do after I'm either done painting or you're done jacking off?" I squeaked.

"Well, you know how most guys reach climax," he paused and looked over his shoulder as he squeezed a tube of paint onto the palette, "and they aren't able to continue?"

I nodded my head and attempted to swallow. I opened my mouth and released an almost audible *yes*. Although I knew what I was trying to say, I was quite certain Jak heard nothing.

"Well, after I cum I'm going to prove a point. I'm going to fuck you until one of us either cums, gives up, or collapses. My guess is I'll do none of the above," he smiled.

Holy.

Fuck.

He picked up my laptop, opened it, and carried it to where I stood, "Unlock this, please."

With shaking hands, I logged onto my computer as he stood beside me in his boxer shorts. I was so aroused I could barely think. After steadying the laptop, he grabbed my hair in his free hand and pulled it into a tight ponytail. As he balanced it in front of me, I saw my sexually frustrated face on the screen. He had obviously activated my web cam. As I stared into the lens and attempted not to focus on Jak standing beside me, he pulled my hair taught and breathed into my ear.

"Smile, Karter. When you like what you see, take a pic. It's what you're going to be painting in a moment. And every time I look at the painting, I'm going to think of stroking my big cock and cumming all over you while you were painting it," his warm breath and the thought of him cumming on me caused my knees to buckle.

KARTER

Oh my fuck.
Shit.
Iamawetfuckingmess.

I turned my head to the right and exposed the left side of my face to the camera. With Jak still pulling my hair tight, I opened my eyes wide and lowered my chin. I moved the cursor and tapped my shaking index finger on the *right click* button. Instantly, a likeness of my face appeared on the screen. Jak released my hair and admired the photo over my shoulder.

"You're gorgeous, Karter," he growled into my ear.

I swallowed the lump in my throat and attempted to straighten my shaking knees. I felt my pussy dripping down my inner thighs. There was no way I'd last a minute with Jak. Not now. I was ready to cum and we hadn't even started yet. As I stood and allowed my mind to float away to thoughts of Jak punishing me sexually, he took the computer from my hands and lowered it to the floor in front of me. Still bent at the knees, he removed his boxers and tilted the screen of the computer rearward as far as he could. As he clutched his cock in his right hand, he pointed to the palette with his left.

"Get busy painting. Remember, don't focus on me, keep painting until I cum, and stay quiet," he demanded as he began to stroke his cock.

I bent over and picked up a brush and the palette. I desperately wanted Jak to fuck me. Now sitting cross legged on the floor beside the computer, Jak began to work his clenched fist up and down the shaft of his massive cock. I glanced at the screen of the computer, studied the photo of my face, and watched as Jak slowly stroked himself. After becoming slightly more uncomfortably aroused, I began to paint.

As I painted my depiction of the photo on the screen, Jak began to tease me. He stood from the floor, walked to my side, and continued working his hand against his cock. It took every bit of reservation I could gather to focus on the screen and not glance at Jak as he masturbated. Eventually, he sat on the floor beside the laptop and sighed heavily.

"You know Karter, I could stroke this big cock of mine all day. I've got seventeen years of practice. But there's something about looking at you that makes me horny as absolute fuck," he leaned forward and positioned his face a matter of inches from my thighs.

I'd had never heard Jak say *fuck* that I could recall. Seeing him like this was a huge turn on. I lifted my left foot and spread my feet shoulder width apart in hopes of *something*. Jak's face now inches from my crotch, he looked upward, "It could be the fact your pussy is dripping down your leg. Are you horny, Karter? Do you want me to fuck you?"

Christ on a cracker, Jak. Fuck me already.

I nodded my head and considered responding, but knew Jak would be upset if I did. I opted to simply nod my head. He raised his chin slightly and licked the length of my pussy as he continued to stroke himself. My knees weakened and I struggled to remain standing. As his tongue touched me again, it stopped along my clit. Softly, he began to suck my swollen nub. I closed my eyes and mentally begged for him to fuck me. As my body began to tingle, I opened my eyes. Squatted at my feet with his eyes closed, Jak worked feverously on his cock as his tongue tortured my pussy.

Please Jak, I'm dying.

I shifted my gaze to the easel. I slopped paint from the palette to the canvas like a mad woman. In the confusion of him stroking his cock and sucking my clit, I'd forgotten our plan. If I could finish painting, we were going to start fucking. Like a woman possessed, I smeared paint on the canvas. Slowly, the painting began to come together. As I continued to attempt to focus on my work, my pussy ached and my spine tingled. I fought against each and every orgasm as they heightened. Eventually, Jak began to moan.

Please, Jak.

Don't...

Moan.

"I think I'm ready to fuck you, Karter," he groaned.

"I'm going to cum so we can get busy fucking," he breathed.

I closed my eyes. His breathing became choppy and labored. I opened my eyes and looked down. I no more than caught a glimpse of Jak's swollen cock, and he opened his eyes and began to slowly stand. Immediately, I looked up and tried to study the canvas.

Please, Jak...

"Get on your knees, Karter," he bellowed.

Thank you.

With the palette still in my hand, I dropped to my knees like a female Tim Tebow preparing for a prayer. My ass hit the backs of my ankles and I opened my mouth. As I felt his cock against my lips, I began to moan. As his swollen shaft slid in and out of my watering mouth, I pressed my tongue against the bottom of his cock. After several strokes, he began to press the tip against my back of my throat. If the possibility existed to die from the anticipation of sex alone, I was mere seconds from the grave. As I felt his cock swell in my throat, I prayed for him to cum in my mouth and regain the strength to fuck me senseless. As Jak began to groan, I moaned against his cock. As his warm cum filled my mouth and throat, I mentally exhaled, knowing what was next. I felt his hands against my armpits and I attempted to stand. As my legs shook from emotional exhaustion, he lifted me to my feet.

He removed the palette and brush from my hand and placed them on the table beside the easel. As he leaned toward me, I closed my eyes in anticipation of a certain kiss. Our lips met, and my knees went weak again. As he held the weight of my body from collapsing on the floor, he kissed my lips with a passion I had never known. My head began to spin in circles. He hadn't even begun to fuck me and I was done. I closed my eyes and remembered his earlier instructions. *I'm going to fuck you until one of us either cums, gives up, or collapses.* This was a contest I had no business being entered in. I was way out of my league with Jak.

As he pulled his lips from mine, he studied my face. Full of desire and lustful thoughts, I stared into his eyes. I loved Jak with every ounce of my existence. After experiencing a life with Jak, attempting for one moment to live without him would be impossible. In Jak's presence, every individual fault I believed existed within me forged together, allowing me to become a strong capable woman. Jak was the answer to a lifetime of me questioning my very own existence.

I felt his wet fingertips glide across my stomach. I blinked my eyes and looked down. His hands covered in the paint from my palette, I watched as he smeared a colorful array of oil onto my skin. He grinned as he raised the paint covered board to my chest. He nodded his head and tilted it slightly. I reluctantly reached for the paint, fully expecting to be reprimanded. He smiled as I pressed my fingers into the reds, blues, and yellow. I rubbed the paint onto my free hand and smiled. Without speaking, I pressed my stomach to his and reached behind him. With both hands, I squeezed his muscular ass in my fingers and wiped the paint against his tight skin. As I held his butt firm in my grip, he began to kiss me again.

KARTER

As my mind became lost in the kiss, my pussy reminded me of the deprivation and torture it had witnessed for the last hour. My entire body began to tingle. I needed Jak inside of me desperately. I released his right butt cheek and slid my hand to his crotch. As I blindly fumbled to find his cock, he pulled his hips from me slightly. I gripped the half stiff shaft into my hand and squeezed as I bit his lower lip.

You're going to fuck me, Jak. And you're going to fuck me now.

I released his lip from my teeth and lowered myself to my knees. As I took his paint covered cock into my mouth the bitter taste of the paint heightened my already overly aroused state. As I worked the shaft into my mouth, I squeezed his ass in my hands. Slowly and methodically, I worked my mouth back and forth as he groaned. The louder he groaned, the more aggressive I became. The further I forced him into my throat, the louder he moaned. As his paint covered hands gripped the sides of my head, he attempted to lift me to my feet.

I buried his now rigid cock deep in my throat, I growled. He moaned as he squeezed my head in his hands and lifted half-heartedly on my jaw. He wanted me to consider stopping, but he loved it when I sucked his cock. I slid my mouth to the rim of the head and flicked my tongue against the tip. I opened my eyes and gazed at the floor. After finding the palette, I reached for my brush and gripped it tightly in my hand. I forced my mouth along the shaft until he was buried in my throat. As I held my mouth against his throbbing nine inches, I raised the brush to his balls and began to tickle the bottom of his scrotum. His legs immediately quivered.

You like that, Jak?

Fuck me you sexy beast.

I attempted to bury his cock deeper in my throat and ran the soft bristles from his balls up and along the crack of his ass. Back and forth the brush slowly stroked as I began to work my mouth along his swollen and slobber covered cock. I slid my mouth from the tip of his cock and wrapped my wet lips around his paint covered balls and began to suck lightly. As I softly began to lose myself in working my tongue against his cleanly shaven scrotum, his hands formed tightly around my neck.

"Time to change it up," he growled.

Against my will and better judgment, he lifted me to my feet. Ultimately, he was going to give me what I wanted – or at least I hoped he was. As I stood and attempted to focus in somewhat of a sexually deprived trance, he lifted me from my feet and began walking across the floor of the apartment. I wrapped my arms around his neck and closed my eyes. As he came to a stop, I opened my eyes. We were in the bathroom. My mind began to run through the possible scenarios.

Bath?

Shower?

Get cleaned up and then start fucking?

He lowered me to the floor and reached into the shower and turned on the water. He motioned toward the enclosure with his hand, "Get in."

I stepped into the shower and closed my eyes as the warm water beat against my hypersensitive body. I opened my eyes as I felt Jak climb in behind me. Without speaking, he reached for my body wash and squeezed it onto my loofah. As I felt the sponge against my skin and inhaled a hint of the floral scent, I closed my eyes. I shivered as the soap filled sponge pressed against my breasts and slid down my torso and between my legs. As his hand pressed into my inner thighs, I felt his cock against the back of my butt cheek. I opened my eyes and pressed my hands against the inner shower wall as I arched my back and lifted

KARTER

myself on my tip-toes.

I want it, Jak.

I need...

I bit my lower lip as his cock pressed into me. His hands slid along my wet soapy body as his hips began to slap against my ass. As the hot water beat against my skin, his hands pressed against my breasts firmly, lifting me from being bent over to standing erect. He dragged his teeth along my neck as he turned me away from the warm water and against the center of the shower's inner structure. With my face against the tile wall, he lifted me slightly with each stroke of his cock. He reached for the shower head and repositioned it to spray the hot water against my right side. Clutched in his arms with his forearms along my torso and his hands squeezing my breasts, he forced himself in and out of me like a man possessed. The angle and the pressure of his cock against my g-spot drove me insane. I was done. I stood on my toes and stretched my calves. He pressed harder against me.

Now forcefully pounding himself in and out of my swollen mound, Jak was proving a point. Age had nothing to do with anything at this juncture. Jak could out-fuck me, outlast me, and out run me. As my wet body slid up and down the surface of the tile wall – literally being lifted from my feet by his cock, I felt myself begin to climax. My head became a whirlwind of meaningless thoughts. I blinked my eyes and stared at the wall.

What the fuck is happening?

His cock worked some type of Navy SEAL magic against my civilian pussy. I felt myself clench against the shaft of his cock. This was going to be huge. As he continued to press deeper into me, my body went limp against the wall. My head exploded into every thought and feeling I had ever encountered in a lifetime of feelings – all at once. I opened my mouth. It happened again. He held himself deep inside of me and began to scream. As his voice echoed throughout the shower and bathroom, his cock swelled. I held my breath and waited as he lifted me from the floor of the shower and against the wall. I exhaled loudly as he exploded his warmth inside of me.

He continued to scream a cry of love, passion, and of proving he could cum twice in one sexual setting. My mind and body expanded into a time and place like no other. I felt as if I had become immortal. A tingling sensation filled me as I flattened my face into the wet wall and reached a level of climactic pleasure I was certain so very few have ever known.

Jak Anderson Kennedy was not the man of my dreams. I never dreamed of wanting a man before I met Jak. Jak happened into my life not as a gift or an answer to one of life's many unanswered questions. I had lived my life as a fractured soul; a misguided and uncertain form of human life with no direction. Assembled of a thousand small pieces of what would never become one, I was truly broken. A large piece of me was missing. No more useful than a clock without its hands, I was incomplete. I needed something to snap into place and allow me to become whole. Try as I might to force something into the empty space within me, I lived a life in denial of my brokenness. Jak was not a compliment to my life, or an object of my desire.

Jak was the last remaining piece of *me*.

He tucked the towel into my cleavage and lifted me from my feet. Exhausted and filled with love, I sighed as Jak carried me into the bedroom. After lowering me to the bed, he pushed his hands onto his hips as I relaxed onto my back. With a towel around his waist and droplets of water covering his muscular body, Jak stood before me smiling.

You torturous prick.

Without speaking, he leaned over me and removed a pillow from the bed. Now standing beside me clutching the corner of the pillow, he grinned as it hung heavily from his grip. Eventually, after a few very long moments of admiring Jak, my eyes fell closed.

Whack!

I felt a dull abrupt pressure against my stomach. I opened my eyes. He swung the pillow again.

Whack!

"Tired?" he howled.

Still not quite mentally competent, I blinked my eyes.

Whack!

"Too exhausted to fight back?" he asked as he raised the pillow over his head.

In what I'm sure Jak would describe as an evasive maneuver, I rolled away from him repeatedly, and grabbed a pillow as I fell to the floor.

The feather pillows were cheap ones from Target, and leaked feathers terribly. Of a typical morning, there would be a dozen feathers littering the floor from just sleeping on them. They were, however, simply lovely to sleep with. As I rose from my squatted position and peered over the top of the comforter, Jak leaped onto the bed. As his body bounced into position, I swung the pillow toward his head.

Whack!

My towel fell to the floor. As he looked down at the bed and attempted to recover, I gripped the pillow with both hands and swung with all my might. Heavily, it came down on the back of his head.

Whack!

"Did that feel like a tired woman swung it?" I screamed as I ran naked into the living room.

Jak immediately followed behind me.

We chased each other through the living room naked for fifteen minutes. No one won and no one lost. Me sitting on one couch and Jak sitting on the other, we each held the pillows against our naked bodies. White feathers filled the air. Jak was a gorgeous man in ways no one would ever know. As Jak stared at me admiringly, I stood, dropped my pillow onto the couch, and walked naked to the easel. After a few minutes of cleanup and preparation, I began to paint. I grinned as I painted a few white feathers in contrast to the purples, blues, and reds surrounding my face. After what seemed like only a matter of minutes, the room began to darken. I looked out the window. The setting sun was all I needed to see to bring me to the realization several hours had passed. I stood back and admired my finished work. Typically, I would sign my first name in the lower right hand corner. If Jak was going to hang this in his apartment, I preferred everyone who entered his home to know who I was. I proudly wanted to claim Jak and bring attention to the fact he was mine.

I squeezed yellow paint onto the palette, and dobbed the brush into it heavily. In four inch tall yellow letters across the bottom of the painting, I stroked my name.

Karter

I turned to face the couch. Naked and partially covered with the pillow, Jak slept. I lifted the painting from the easel and quietly carried it to the couch opposite where Jak slept. I leaned the freshly painted canvas against the cushion so he could see it when he woke up. I lifted my pillow from the floor and walked toward Jak. Softly, I lowered myself onto the couch beside him and pressed my skin to his. As I pulled the pillow to my body for a little warmth, I looked across the room at my work.

I looked beautiful.

The bold yellow name across the bottom of the painting would make clear to anyone who entered his apartment who I was.

Stay away bitch, he's mine.

JAK

A three month anniversary may be nothing measurable to most people, but to me it was as significant as landing on the moon. Karter was scheduled to leave town and make an appearance at an art exhibit in Dallas, Texas over the weekend. Although I would have loved to accompany her, the tight schedule for the event and the fact my mother's air conditioner was broken would prevent me from going with her. We agreed the two days away from each other would serve the two of us as a reminder of the depth of our love and affection for each other.

Soon it would be fall, and the outdoor activities would shrink as the weather cooled and the days became shorter. As strange as it seemed to say, I looked forward to autumn and winter with Karter. Spending time with her in her home made me feel as if we were an actual couple. Having a life with her outside of eating, movies, and social activities would be satisfying on an entirely different level. Having a home life with Karter would satisfy me greatly.

The waitress smiled as she removed our plates from the table. Karter sat back in the booth and sighed as she rubbed her stomach. *Adrian's* had become our preferred place to eat out. Having felt guilty for leaving before we actually ate the first time, we soon returned. The meal was fabulous, and the service was second to none. Each time I asked Karter where she wanted to eat, she rolled her eyes and shook her head.

KARTER

Adrian's.

Nervously, I leaned into the center of the table, "So are you excited about this weekend?"

"No. I'm damned near sick about it. Do you realize since the day we met, the very first day, we haven't spent so much as one day apart?" she shrugged.

I was well aware. To think of her being away from me caused me to feel uneasy. Karter had not become a part of my life or even my significant other; I needed her to simply survive. To dream of being without Karter was not to think of being alone, but to think of not even being. Karter had become my life support system.

"I'm well aware. That's what makes your weekend good and bad both. It'll be good for us," I sighed.

"Whatever. Good for you. Fine. Speak for yourself. It's going to kill me. I hate to even think of doing this. I used to love art shows. Stupid fuckers will come up to me for the entire weekend and hit on me. They always do. I'll just tell them I'm spoken for," she sighed.

I swallowed a lump which had developed in my throat and reached into my pocket. As I pulled my hand out and rested it into my lap, I took a shallow breath. She was shaking her head lightly and looking around the restaurant as if the thought of being away disgusted her. I reached my cupped hand over the center of the table and curled my index finger toward my palm. At some point in time, each and every time we ate at *Adrian's*, this had become my signature. Me motioning her to the center of the table to whisper in her ear and kiss her. As Karter smiled and leaned into the edge of the table, I moved forward in my seat and met her in half way. I puckered my lips and closed my eyes slightly. As her soft mouth met mine and we embraced in a shallow kiss, my body tingled from head to toe.

She's the one, Jak.

The only one.

I uncupped my hand and pointed into my palm, "Wear this if you'll honor me by doing so. It may keep them away for a little more than the weekend."

The diamond engagement ring glistened in the dimly lit lighting of the restaurant. She looked into my hand and stared.

"Jak?" she raised her hands slowly to her cheeks.

"Jak?"

I swallowed heavily again and looked up, "What I feel for you defines love in the purest sense, Karter. It's inevitable. We're destined to spend our lives together, forever. Begin forever with me. Karter Wilson, will you marry me?"

The words came easier than I expected. Karter reached toward my palm and hesitated. As she looked at me, her eyes glistened. They were brown tonight with green specs, her natural color. Slowly, her mouth formed a smile of deep satisfaction. Her fingers hovered over my open hand. As reassurance, I nodded my head slightly. She carefully pinched the ring between her thumb and forefinger and held it in her hand.

"If it's not what you were expecting…"

"Just stop," she sighed as she wiped the back of her free hand against her eyes.

"Yes. Shit Jak, I'm sorry. I forgot to answer. Yes. Fuck yes, I'll marry you. That's the dumbest question I've ever heard. Will I? Jesus. I was placed on this earth for you. You and I both know it. Now aren't you supposed to put this big fucker on my finger?" her voice cracked as she attempted to speak.

I reached out and took the ring from between her fingers and pinched it between my thumb and forefinger. As she leveled her shaking hand over the center of the table, I raised my eyebrows and slid the ring onto her finger, "So it's a yes?"

"Yes," she sighed as she looked down at the ring.

The best and the worst life offers are separated in our mind as differing memories by our brain's ability to recollect them accurately. Our mind simply categorizes the various events. In a mission in one of Africa's small countries, we were dropped onto the roof of a large compound. It was to be a simple extraction of a military official who believed genocide was the answer to the countries level of poverty.

As I entered the window of the upper floor, a young man no more than eighteen reached for an AK-47. My training and experience took over and I reacted. A single round entered his skull above the brow line. He was fifteen feet from me. In the very well lit room, I watched as his head exploded. It was my first kill. My mind recalled the memory of it nightly until I killed my second. By the time I had so many kills I was either incapable of counting or no longer felt the need, I stopped recalling it on a steady or daily basis. It still lingered with me, as it should. It now lingers, however, as a memory. Without a doubt, the first person I killed was the saddest day of my life.

The best, and arguably the proudest day of my life had been the day I graduated BUD/S training and became a Navy SEAL.

Until now.

Karter accepting the request to become my wife far exceeded any level of pride I had ever felt or could ever expect to feel again. Comprehending her allowing me to be her husband was close to impossible. For now, I chose to simply accept it and wallow in the thought of her being for me as good as I knew I'd be for her.

"I love you," I smiled.

"Jak, you have no idea how happy I am," she said as she looked down at the ring.

"I've got to pee," she smiled.

As I watched her walk toward the bathroom in her signature Karter stroll, I felt an odd relief of my life being in order. A certain fear prior to retiring from the Navy caused me to look at my retirement day as a curse, and not a blessing. Visions of depression, guilt, and becoming another PTSD suicide statistic filled my mind. Now, watching Karter walk away, nothing could be further from the truth.

"Jak Kennedy!" an unfamiliar man's voice exclaimed.

No one here should know me.

Shocked, I turned to my left and stood in a somewhat defensive posture.

"Damn, killer. Settle down. Just thought I'd say hi. You don't remember me, do you?" he asked.

I studied his face. I had no idea who he may be.

"Pete Townsend?" he said softly as he pointed at his face and smiled.

I shook my head.

"*Little Petey*? I was a couple years younger than you in school."

The last thing I wanted was to see someone from school. Those memories were long since passed and I wanted to keep them forgotten. In an effort to be kind, I smiled.

"I vaguely remember. I'm sorry, nice to see you," I said as I extended my hand and shook his lightly.

"So, you and Shelley's daughter out for dinner? She's kind of young for you ain't she?" he chuckled.

My head began to spin. My face felt hot. I was becoming confused. "Shelley?" I muttered.

"Yeah, Shelley Peterson. Hell, you used to date her back in the day, didn't you? Before you became a Marine or whatever?" he said as he slapped my shoulder.

My heart began to race. *Shelley Peterson.* The last name I wanted to hear, and the primary reason I would never return to my hometown. But Karter's last name was Wilson and she was from Connecticut. He was clearly confused. I swallowed the lump in my throat and intended on ending the conversation quickly. As I reached for my wallet, removed a hundred dollar bill and dropped it onto the table, he continued.

"Hell, I hadn't seen her since she was a kid. Maybe five years ago, when she left her mom and moved from town. Her mom's nuttier than a fuckin' fruitcake, so it was no surprise she left her like that," he chuckled.

I looked up from the bill I dropped on the table and blinked my eyes.

Focus Jak.

"Well, it was nice seeing you again, Petey. I've got to get," I said as I slapped his shoulder and turned toward the rear of the restaurant.

Appearing somewhat confused, he shrugged and smiled, "Alrighty. Nice seein' ya."

As I briskly walked to the rear of the restaurant, my head began to spin. If what he said was true I...

It can't be true Jak, think. It's impossible.

I shook my head and attempted to think of times and dates. My head slowly became a fog of memories, events, and faces I had long since forgotten. As Karter stepped from the bathroom and smiled, visions of my high school prom filled my head.

And I began to feel ill.

JAK

"The air conditioner is fixed, it was the contactor," I said as I walked into the kitchen.

"Well, it doesn't *feel* fixed. I'll call the repairman," my mother complained as she snuffed her cigarette out.

"Mom, it's fixed. It's fine. Close the windows and it'll be cool in here in a few minutes," I sighed as I walked to the bathroom.

I washed my hands and looked into the mirror. I felt all of the things I expected to feel with retirement, but reserved hope I wouldn't. Standing and looking at my reflection, a different man looked back at me. I was tired, lonely, depressed, angry, ashamed, and unwilling to accept my past was coming back to haunt me. I felt mentally mixed up and I was physically ill. Although my mind was a mess, I needed to do my best to mask it and determine just what was going on in my life before something terrible happened.

Something even I could not resolve.

I leaned into the kitchen slightly. My mother remained sitting at the table with the windows still opened and the air conditioning blowing full force.

"Mom, where's my box of stuff from the old house? The one I kept all my high school stuff in?"

"I put it up," she snapped.

"Where, mom?" I sighed.

"You don't need to go digging in that box. Graham's gone Jak. Don't go digging him up," she said softly.

I tried to tell myself I didn't hear her, but my mind began to race again. Since Karter and I left the restaurant, I hadn't slept. Recounting past events and memories, my mind began to question everything. I had some things I must do, and if what I hoped to be a mistake proved to be true, my only resolution would be to leave this city and never turn back or...

Become a PTSD statistic.

"Mom, where is it. I just want to look at a photo, and then I've got to run. I'll be back in a few days," I lied.

"I put it downstairs. It's in the spare bedroom with everything else. Don't go upsetting yourself, Jak. When's Karter coming home?"

"In a few days, mom. Alright. I'll say goodbye on my way out."

I ran down the stairs and into the spare bedroom. In the corner of the room was a large light green wooden chest. I knelt at the front of the chest and took a deep breath. As I opened the box I saw the photo album on top, right where I hoped it would be. Without opening it, I removed it, tucked it under my arm, and stared into the chest.

Hundreds of unopened letters filled the chest. Stacks and stacks of bound envelopes side by side filled the majority of the box. For the first two years of training, I had sent each and every letter home, unopened. The only mail I opened or responded to was from my mother. In my opinion, considering all things at the time, reading anything from friends would only cause me grief and potentially diminish my chances of successfully completing my training. As I stared at the stacks of letters, I wondered now what they may contain. Frustrated and unwilling to attempt to relive my entire past, I shut the lid to the chest.

I stood in the doorway and looked into the room as if I expected some form of response from the within the chest. I needed answers, and to get them I was going to go where I felt I had no business being. It wasn't going to be a comfortable situation, but it had to be done. As much as I didn't want to know, I knew I had to find the answers. Without knowing the truth, I couldn't continue to live with Karter in my life, or even alone for that matter. I flipped off the light and turned from the room.

"Mom, I grabbed a few photo's. I'm going to home for a bit and then I may have to go meet Commander Warrenson," I said from the top of the stairs.

"You retired, Jak. Why do you have to go see him? Why Jak? And come give me a kiss. Since when do you leave without kissing me? What's wrong with you, Jak?" my mother whined.

I placed the photo album on the floor and stepped over it and into the kitchen. As my mother scowled at me, I wrapped my arms around her and held her. She was the only woman I felt I could truly trust.

"I love you, mom," I breathed.

"I love you too, Jak. What's going on?" she asked.

"Nothing mom. I just saw a guy last night and he made me think of a few things. It's not about Graham. I just wanted to see a few people. Nothing to worry about," I assured her.

"Alright. Well as soon as Karter gets back, you two come over here for dinner, okay?"

I hope so, mom. I sure hope so.

"I'll let you know," I said as I turned toward the stairs.

"*I'll let you know* if you don't straighten up, Jak," she huffed.

KARTER

I grabbed the album and walked to my truck. I opened the door, and tossed it into the front seat. I gripped the keys in my hand and inhaled a deep breath. I really didn't want to do this, but I knew I had to. It wasn't quite thirty miles to Potwin, and even in my old truck shouldn't take thirty minutes.

The longest thirty minutes of my life.

JAK

If Bin Laden couldn't hide in Pakistan, Shelley Peterson couldn't expect to remain hidden in a town of 900 people. After asking the local cashier at the only gas station in the city, I had quickly found her address. Although I didn't know for certain what she was going to do or say, I knew what I expected. This was certainly going to be a reunion I wasn't looking forward to.

I parked the truck a block from where she was supposed to live. It was the same vehicle I had driven since I was in high school, and I feared she'd recognize it if i drove it in clear view of her home. If she did realize it was me visiting, she may not answer the door. I pushed the photo album under the seat and pulled the baseball cap I'd purchased down to my brow. I shut the door, locked the truck, and walked down the street of a neighborhood I had not seen in over twenty years. Reluctantly, I walked up the driveway and onto the porch. After a short pause and prayer, I inhaled a deep breath and knocked on the door. Almost immediately, it opened.

She remained petite and still rather attractive. It was obvious by the look on her face she had no idea who I was. As my heart began to race, and I mentally prepared for the worst, she broke the uncomfortable silence.

"Something I can do for you?" she asked.

KARTER

I reached up and removed the baseball cap, "Shell."

She stared as if she'd seen a ghost. After what seemed like an eternity, she began right where I expected her to, "Jak fucking Kennedy, war hero. You know Jak, it doesn't matter how many people you think you may have saved in that war; you still killed him. Doesn't really matter how long you were away, it'll never change. You need to leave and not be bringing memories back here talking about shit I'm trying to forget."

I took a deep breath and exhaled, "It's not why I'm here, Shell. Can I come in?"

She swung the door opened and turned toward the living room. Hesitantly, I stepped into the house and attempted to settle her down, "Shell. We've been over this. I didn't kill him. It was a motorcycle accident. An absolute accident. Sometimes things happen, and we have no control over them."

"You son-of-a-bitch. Accept it. Admit it. You know I wouldn't hate you if you'd just admit it. You two were drunk and you were racing. If it wasn't for you, he'd still be here," her voice became unsteady and she sat down on the edge of the couch.

Graham, Shelley, and I were best friends since we were ten years old. We were close at a much younger age, but became inseparable in middle school. Shelley and I dated all through high school, and most who knew us expected we would become married. Although in our latter years she had become somewhat unpredictable in her actions, I always believed I loved her. When Graham and I announced our intent to join the Navy and attempt to become SEALS, she was livid. She spent many a long night with Graham attempting to talk him out of going to the Navy. I believed she felt all along if she could stop him form going, it would prevent me from proceeding with my plan to become a SEAL as well.

We remained together up to the point Graham died. She blamed me solely for his accident; and after his funeral we separated. A matter of one day after his funeral, I left for training. She hadn't spoken to me since, nor did I have any expectation of her doing so. Shelley and Graham were like brother and sister, and Graham's death was far more difficult for her to accept than anyone else. No one quite understood the connection between them, or the pain she felt, but I did. She and Graham were like family.

"I'm sorry you feel the way you do about it all, Shell. I suppose I reserved a little hope you'd feel different about it now. I've never refused to believe what happened actually *happened*, but I chose to set the memory of it aside. I guess at least until the other day. I uhhm," I paused and thought of how to word the remaining portion of my question without giving too much information away.

"Graham's bike was green, wasn't it?" I asked.

Since opening the chest and driving to her house, I had begun to remember things about my former life I hadn't remembered in years. If someone would have asked me two weeks prior what color Graham's bike was, I wouldn't have been able to answer. Now, I was recalling things about my early years with each tick of the clock.

"You know what color it was," she growled as she stood from the couch.

"Shell, if I did, I wouldn't have asked. Like I said, it's really difficult for me. I have a hard time remembering any of that part of my life," I said as I stood.

She turned to face me and scowled, "Yes, dark green. Is that why you came here?"

I pulled the ball cap tightly onto my head and crossed my arms, "Not entirely. I thought I saw Graham's old bike the other day, but with a few different parts on it. I wasn't sure. I knew you bought it from his parents after the wreck, but I wasn't sure what you ever did with it."

"It's gone," she grunted.

"Well, is it around here?" I asked.

She shrugged, "Hard sayin', I suppose it could be."

"What did you do with it?" I asked.

"I gave the motherfucker away, Jak. After fifteen years, I couldn't stand to look at it anymore," she snapped.

I better leave that one alone for now.

"You ever get married?" I asked.

She crossed her arms and sighed, "No, and it's none of your business, Jak. Jesus, why'd you come here? To cause me pain? Maybe you should go."

"I just wanted to ask about the bike. It was a Harley, right?" I asked.

"Just stop, Jak. Please," she paused and placed her hands on her hips.

"Why didn't you respond to my letters, Jak?" she sniffed.

"What letters?" I asked

"The letters, Jak. Don't be stupid. I wrote you for a year. You never responded. Maybe once a month for a while, then I wrote once a week for a few months. I never heard from you," she reached toward her cheek and wiped a tear from her face.

"I didn't read any of my letters. Not a one, Shell. I tossed them out. To be honest, I completed the training not so much for me, but for Graham. At least that's what I told myself. I felt if I had any influence from the real world, or felt any of the emotion from all of this, I wouldn't make it through the training. For me, failure wasn't an option. It would have been like I was letting Graham down. He wanted me to be a SEAL as bad as I wanted it. So if you wrote me, I'm sorry. I never read them," I said shamefully.

I truly began to feel sorry for Shelley. More than twenty years had passed and she was still in the same place mentally as she was when I left. Regardless, I needed answers. No matter what her response was, I was quite certain considering all things I'd never see her again. She hated me anyway, and I was ready to bring this visit to a close.

"I heard you had a daughter," I said softly as I turned toward the door.

Her face covered with wonder, she responded, "Who told you that? I thought you didn't read the letters?"

"I didn't Shell. I saw a guy in town, Little Petey. He said you had a daughter. What's your daughter's name, Shell?" I asked over my shoulder as I approached the door.

"Her name's Karter, Jak. She changed her last name," she said angrily.

Facing the door, I heard her begin to cry. As I stood and contemplated leaving, she said one more thing. One single thing that changed everything, "Jak she's *our* daughter."

My heart sank. My head spun. This couldn't be. She was twenty one. I was thirty-eight. I wouldn't be thirty nine for another five months. I joined the Navy when I was I was seventeen, in January 1993. Karter's age made it almost impossible for her to be...

Fuck.

It was possible. It was probable. It began to make sense. I turned to face Shell. I felt hot. I began to shiver. I turned toward the doorway. My stomach convulsed.

KARTER

"Yeah, Jak. You have a daughter."
And I vomited.

JAK

"Jak I don't know how I'm going to help you, I really don't," he sighed from across the large living room.

"Commander, this isn't something I want. I *need* this. I just hopped on a commercial bird and flew here from Kansas. I haven't slept in almost thirty six hours. This is critical," I shouted.

He began to plead, "Jak, I'd love to help, I'm just afraid…"

I was a degree of angry I had never known. The thought of the woman I deeply loved being my daughter was something I was currently incapable of comprehending or dealing with. The pain I felt when I considered *not* spending my life with Karter was enough to bring me to the brink of suicide. Daughter or not, I loved Karter. I loved her even now. Try as I might, I could not change how I felt.

The crushing pain weighing down on my breaking heart far exceeded the guilt and self-imposed blame from all of the men I had killed combined. Denying she was my daughter didn't change anything. Over the last twelve hours, I attempted to accept the fact she was my daughter. All of the events began to make sense. As a matter of fact, it was almost undeniable. Karter was my daughter. I forced myself to believe it, yet I still loved her with all of my being. Now filled with tremendous guilt for loving the woman I had planned on spending a lifetime loving and cherishing caused me to feel ill. Feeling ill for loving her made me angry. I loved Karter and it was beginning to infuriate me.

The anger built up inside of me.

And I eventually exploded.

"Afraid? You're afraid? The first time we went into Wardak province. The first fucking time," I screamed.

He stepped back two steps and looked as me as if he believed I was insane.

"Who the fuck was the first one to volunteer?" I bellowed.

His face was filled with worry, "Jak. It's just..."

"I wasn't done speaking, Commander. Who was first?" I demanded as I began to walk closer to him.

He raised his hands to his chest and turned his palms toward me as if to slow my approach, "You were Jak."

"You're fucking right, I was. Now, do you recall how many confirmed kills I had on that mission alone? How many, Commander?" I shouted as I continued to walk his direction slowly.

"Jak..."

"Four. Four confirmed. You want to know about the kills not on the report, sir? Do you? Do you think I was scared?" I tossed my bag onto the floor and looked up.

"Kandahar province. 2007. When I caught that bullet in the back of my thigh. What the fuck did I do?" I growled.

"Jak, this isn't about..."

"What. The. Fuck. Did. I. Do?" I growled.

"Jak I don't remember..."

"You can't remember? Well, I'll never fucking forget. With all due respect, the fuck you don't remember, Commander. What did I do?"

He took a deep breath, stared down at the floor, and sighed, "You dug the bullet out with your blade and refused treatment so you could go back in," he sighed.

The anger began to mount within me. I nodded my head and crossed my arms, "Kunar province back in 2006, when we went in to save those Marines from being ambushed. Who carried three of those poor boys down that mountain? Do *you* sir, remember that? I sure as absolute fuck didn't carry them all down at once, either. Remember? I went up and motherfucking down the mountain, taking fire with each trip up and each respective trip down sir. Over and fucking over as I was shot at by a hundred Al Qaeda."

I recalled receiving the Silver Star for my bravery in carrying the wounded Marines down the mountain from the ambush site. *Gallantry in action against an enemy of the United States.* My eyes began to well with tears.

I took the last step which separated us and tightened my jaw muscles. My voice elevated even higher, "Who earned the Silver Star in that mission alone? Over almost twenty-one years sir, I was awarded the Silver Star, Bronze Star, six Purple Hearts..."

"Jak, alright. You made your point. Exactly what do you need and when?" he asked as he raised his hands between our chests.

"It isn't about making my point, *sir.* It's about sacrifice. I sacrificed everything. And although ultimately it was for the country, I did it because *you* asked me to. *You.* Now, the time has come for me to request a service from *you.* I'm asking you to pull a few strings, not break laws. Are we understood, sir?"

I was exhausted and angry. He took a few shallow breaths and looked into my eyes, "What Jak? What and when?"

"I already told you, I need a DNA test," I sighed as I turned away and reached for my bag.

He exhaled loudly, "What type of timeframe are we talking about?"

"I need it by tomorrow," I said as I pulled the two marked envelopes from the bag.

"Tomorrow?" he complained.

"You and I both know it takes less than twenty-four hours. Like I said Commander, pull a few strings," I grunted as I tossed the envelopes on the couch beside where he stood.

He crossed his arms, "If it's siblings or distant…"

"It's father-daughter. A simple test," I said as I tossed the two envelopes on the couch beside where he stood.

"You in some kind of a mess, Jak?" he asked.

"Have the test performed, sir. I'll be back in the morning," I sighed.

KARTER

I pushed the phone into my pocket. I felt ill. I hadn't heard from Jak in two days. One simple apologetic text message from him explaining his Commander called and he would be *out of pocket* for a week was all I had received since I left for the art show. On the night he proposed to me in the restaurant, something changed while I was in the bathroom. When I came back to the table, he was different. At first I thought he was nervous or having second thoughts, but it wasn't that. He was hurting, I could tell. He didn't say so at that point in time, but his Commander called while I was in the restroom. Now with Jak absent, the remark he made when he left bounced around in my head.

I love you Karter, and I always will. Nothing on this earth will ever change that.

It now caused me to worry about where he was and what he was doing.

Jak believed the separation from each other would cause us to understand the depth of our love. I needed no lesson to understand the love I felt for Jak. My connection to him was clear since the first day we met. The time we spent together did nothing but confirm what I already knew. Jak and I were tied together by a force much greater than the love most people feel for each other. Jak and I had something no one else did. Jak and I were somehow fused together as one.

KARTER

Simply stated, I needed Jak to survive. Now standing at an art show with three hundred idiots wandering around looking at the artwork displayed in the exhibit, I felt as if I was dying. Without Jak, I struggled to breathe. My every thought included Jak in some way. I wondered where he was, if he was in danger, what he was eating, if he was thirsty, why he couldn't text me, if he was in this country or if he had left. I wondered if he was being shot at or would be required to defend his life.

I never asked, and he never offered, but the scars on his body obviously weren't from accidents as a child. They were from being shot. If Jak had escaped death as many times as I expected he had, in time the laws of average would catch up to him. The thought of losing Jak consumed me. Without Jak in my life, there would be no life. Without Jak I would die.

"So are you Karter?" A man in his mid-thirties asked.

"Say again?" I snapped.

Fuck, I sound like Jak.

"Karter? The artist? Are you Karter?"

I smiled a shitty grin and nodded. I was far from in the mood to chat.

"I love your tattoos," he grinned.

You fucking idiot.

I raised my hand in the air and pushed against the edge of my engagement ring with my thumb, rotating the large diamond to the front of my hand, "Are you blind or just fucking stupid? See this?"

He shrugged and looked half embarrassed.

"My Navy SEAL fiancé gave me this. You know why?"

He scoffed, turned, and began to walk away.

"To keep fuck-sticks like you from hitting on me," I barked.

The emotional cloud I was floating on the night Jak proposed to me was took me to a place higher than I had ever been. To be elevated to that height, to feel the degree of warmth from the love Jak and I shared, only to be dropped into the depth of the pit I was in now caused me to feel ill.

If something's happened to Jak, I'll just die

I reached into my back pocket and pulled out my phone. I swiped my finger across the screen. *Please.* I pressed the text message icon. *Please.*

Nothing.

"Karter, there's someone over here who would like to talk to you about your work," Mr. Weinburg smiled as he finished speaking.

Frustrated, I pushed my phone into my pocket. Wearing a dress and heels made me angry in the first place, but wearing a dress and heels without Jak present made me even more disappointed. I tried to force a smile as I nodded and followed him across the floor.

"You must be Karter," the man sighed as he extended his hand, "I'm Stephen Greene."

He was dressed in a suit. It appeared he must have spent as much money having it tailored as he did buying it in the first place. And from the looks of the suit, it was by no means inexpensive. I looked down at his perfectly polished shoes and slowly up to his overly tanned face.

I smiled and reached for his hand, "The one and only."

"I've perused the entire exhibit and everything I see which draws me in close has the same name at the bottom right corner. Would you like to guess who?" he grinned.

I was in no mood to play idiotic games with stupid people. I wanted Jak. I was almost in tears as it was, and I don't ever cry. Frustrated and desperately needing to feel Jak's strong arms around me, I opened my mouth and spoke my mind.

"I'm not in a good mood. To be quite honest, I feel like I may puke. If you have something to say, say it. If not, I'm going to go to the bathroom," I said in a soft yet stern tone.

Mr. Weinburg placed his hand on my shoulder and stepped between Mr. Greene and I, "Do you have any idea who he is?"

"I don't care," I whispered.

He cupped his hand to my ear, "Greene Street Studio in New York City, Karter. He *owns* it. He's considering buying all of your art. Everything. Not consignment, he wants to purchase it."

"Well, sell it to him. I feel sick, I'm sorry. And I'm not in the mood to be toyed with. I'm sick and fucking tired of this place and of everyone in it," I complained.

"Karter, you're a talented artist, but you're a poor business woman. He wants to speak to *you.*"

I pulled my face away from his cupped hand and shook my head, "Tell him to follow me to the bathroom. He can watch me take a shit for the fourth time today while we negotiate."

I nodded and smiled toward Mr. Greene and turned toward the elevator. The only thing which would even come close to making me happy would be to either see or hear from Jak. The weekend separated from each other was the worst idea to have ever crossed my mind. As I walked down the hallway, I swore I'd never leave Jak again for any reason.

I love you, Jak.

I need you to pick me up.

And let my legs dangle.

JAK

I stopped the rental car at the end of the driveway and waited for the Commander to arrive. I hadn't slept in forty-eight hours. Regardless of my training and experiences in sleep deprivation, the lack of sleep was wearing on me heavily. I had become even more agitated and short tempered since we had met the previous night. I looked toward the passenger seat at my bag and closed my eyes.

I don't come to you often, but I'm coming to you now. You started this mess, I didn't. You put her in my life. I fought wars behind the shield of your name and your grace. I made it out alive, and not by my will. I prayed for you to take my life.

You chose not to.

I'm telling you now, if you take her from me, I'm not going to pray for you to take me. I'll bow out by my own hand. I'm done with the games. I can't continue. If she's my daughter, the world can't accept me loving her in this way, and I'm incapable of stopping.

It's not a threat Lord, It's a promise. I'm not here to negotiate. I'm here to ask forgiveness in advance.

If Karter was my daughter, I couldn't simply stop loving her. To continue to *actively* love her would be wrong, and contrary to all things I and everyone of this earth held to be moral. Loving her was not something I had chosen to do, but more a transformation which happened within me. I made no conscious choice to make Karter my lover; I merely allowed her access to my heart. She nestled into place naturally, and there she would always remain.

For me to live and *not* love Karter would be impossible. Many people on this earth are of the belief they are currently in love. In due time, most will undoubtedly become bored and wander from their existing love to another person and fall in love all over again. Feeling what *true* love can and does provide allows me to look at those people and their respective relationships with sorrow. I now know true love is not a once in a lifetime blessing, but something only a select few will ever know. Most people on this earth would never experience firsthand the love I felt for Karter.

Therefore, they would not be able to understand why I could not stop loving her.

After tremendous thought and prayer, I decided for me to continue to live on this earth and *not* have Karter as my lover would be impossible. If I was alive and allowed to wander this earth, I realized I would do so with Karter as my lover or not at all.

I watched in the rearview mirror as his car pulled into the driveway. I unzipped my bag and removed the Sig Saur pistol from the holster. As I rested it in my lap, I inhaled a deep breath. I exhaled slowly as his car came to a stop alongside where I was parked. I rolled down my window, and peered in his direction.

He opened the door to his car and began to step out. I gripped the pistol in my hand and placed my finger against the trigger. As he stepped from the car, he began to speak, "I don't know what you were hoping for Jak, but I have the results."

"Stay in the car, Commander," I demanded in a military-esque voice.

He stopped in his tracks, "Kennedy?"

"That's right, Commander. Jak's gone. Kennedy needs an answer, and he needs it now," I demanded.

My hand in my lap and out of view, I gripped the pistol firmly, "Commander?"

"November Oscar, Kennedy. The DNA is not a match," he responded.

I sighed and closed my eyes. I tossed the pistol in the bag and removed two marked envelopes and zipped the bag closed. I held my arm out the window with the envelopes gripped tightly in my hand.

"Kennedy?"

"I'll be back tomorrow," I sighed.

"Kennedy? God damn it..."

I dropped the envelopes onto the concrete drive and shifted the car in reverse, "Same test, same time frame, Commander."

As I backed the car from the drive, I momentarily closed my eyes.

One more thing.

Provide me strength.

KARTER

The fact I was driving the U-Haul van home from Dallas and it was empty of all my art should have made me happy. I was far from it. I had not heard a word from Jak in over two days. *Nothing*. My wallet filled with a forty thousand dollar check and my heart filled with pain, I merged the raggedy assed van onto I-35 North and pushed the gas pedal to the floor.

Painting and riding my motorcycle had become what I called my *escape from reality*. After having Jak in my life, I was able to describe them in a more accurate sense. They were an escape from me. In Jak's presence, I was as close to normal as I suppose I could ever expect to be. In Jak's absence, I was becoming a complete emotional wreck.

I was becoming myself.

As a child, and not having outlets for my discussing my fears or desires, I expressed myself in fits of rage. I often lashed out with cussing and screaming. The curse words became second nature, and as an adult my mouth was as foul as any man. My mother spent all of her time drinking, and she gave very little consideration to me as a child. When I wanted or needed something, I asked. When she didn't respond or appear to care, I often cussed and screamed to get her to pay attention to me.

The attention rarely came.

KARTER

I never quite understood what I may have done to deserve the treatment she gave me. For a mother to all but abandon her daughter mentally and emotionally was one thing. For her to not express any form of love was contrary to what I would have considered to be basic maternal instinct; and something which I found very difficult to accept. When I finally told her I wanted to seek emancipation through the courts, and that I intended to separate myself from her, a small part of me hoped she would oppose the idea.

In my mind, at least at the time, it was a last ditch effort on my part to give her an opportunity to try and make things right between us. She had no interest in doing so, and seemed relieved when I announced my eagerness to leave and begin a life on my own. Even as I explained I had no desire to ever see her or speak to her again, she seemed at peace with my decision.

Almost as if my leaving her was a relief.

I don't miss her. Not even in the least. I had lived my life prior to leaving her alone, and my time away from her was no different. Since the age of sixteen, I had always believed I needed no one to assist me in my journey through the puzzle of life. Jak happening into my life changed my views entirely. Initially, I tried to be standoffish and rude. It lasted all of about an hour. Everything about him provided me with a level of warmth and comfort I never knew existed. I'm sure most women yearn for such a man. I had no idea such feelings existed, as I had never felt them, therefore the desire was never present for me.

Jak had brought so many new thoughts and feelings into my life. Experiencing them and having felt the love Jak filled me with now caused me to yearn for what I had grown accustomed to being provided.

Jak's love.

I glanced at my hand as it rested atop the steering wheel. I tilted it toward me and smiled. The diamond glistened in the sun as the van shimmied down the rough Texas highway. I shifted my gaze to the seat beside me.

Empty.

For an instant I closed my eyes.

Without you Jak, I feel empty and alone.

JAK

I sat in the driveway with the window down. Waiting had never been one of my strengths. I stared into the passenger seat at the photo album from my past. Reluctantly, I opened the cover. My last entry, a series of photographs of Graham and I before and after our pre-Navy haircuts was on the page facing me. On the top of the page, long locks of each of our hair taped against the page with twenty year old Scotch tape. We had each saved them as a reminder of our friendship. Who would have guessed then how useful they would become later. I felt my heart rate increase as the Commander's car slowly entered the drive. As he cautiously inched his vehicle beside me, he rolled his window down and remained in the car.

Resolving the mystery and moving forward with my life was something I felt I desperately needed to allow me to find peace. Attempting to make sense of everything and fully understanding it would certainly be impossible. Proceeding with living life and allowing myself to heal from the wounds of my past would provide me with a comfort twenty years of fighting could not.

"Kennedy, I'm going to remain in the vehicle. I have no idea where your head is right now," he explained as he leaned out of the window.

"Match?" I asked.

He nodded his head.

"Positive?" I asked.

I knew a DNA match would be positive. I needed to hear it.

"That's affirmative, Kennedy. It's a match. Father-daughter, no doubt," he nodded.

"Toss it in the window, Commander," I sighed.

I stared down into my lap. As tears welled in my eyes, I realized I was beginning to cry for more than one reason. Filled with emotion and free of sleep for almost seventy-two hours, I was on the verge of a breakdown; but the tears came naturally from two simultaneous feelings. Love and pain. As the envelopes and a plastic packet landed in the seat beside me, I stared at the thighs of my jeans. His stern voice caused me to look his direction.

"We done here, Kennedy?" he asked.

I cleared my throat. A single tear dripped down my cheek, "Jak, Commander. Remember?"

"Glad you're back, Jak," he said as he opened his car door.

"I've got to hop on a bird and get back to Wichita. This investigation is almost over, but we're done here," I said as he leaned in the window of the car.

Another tear worked its way alongside my nose and collected on my upper lip. Yet another followed. Still focused on me, and never having seen emotion from me whatsoever, his eyes widened.

"Jak, you need a cup of coffee? A place to sleep?" he asked.

"No sir," I responded as I shifted the car in reverse.

"I need to pick a girl up off the floor until her legs dangle," I smiled as I wiped the tears from my eyes.

"Fair enough," he grinned.

He had made the statement many times over the years. I've always said we mimic those we admire. I pressed my foot firmly on the brake and smiled the best I was able.

"Fair enough," I repeated.

As he stood from the car window, I backed out of the driveway. Sitting in the street, I shifted the car into drive and held my foot on the brake as I lifted the DNA test and envelopes from the seat and dropped them into the bag. As difficult as it was for me to accept or understand, I now knew the answer to my little mystery. The top envelope was clearly marked by my hand writing. The name I had scribbled onto it before giving it to the Commander, without a doubt, was Karter's father.

Graham.

JAK

Although it wasn't necessary, I felt I had one more thing to do for my peace of mind. I pulled my ball cap tight onto my head and lowered my gaze to the floor as I walked past the security camera. I really had nothing to hide, but I didn't want Karter to know what I was preparing to do. With the bag over my shoulder now filled with a few tools and a flashlight, I pressed the security code on the keypad. As the magnetic lock on the front door buzzed, I pulled it open and walked to the elevator.

As the elevator door opened into the lower floor parking garage, I stepped around the corner and into Karter's parking stall. Her motorcycle was parked right where she had left it before she went to the art show. As it was two o'clock in the morning, I had very little doubt Karter was doing anything but sleeping - something I clearly needed to join in on, as I had not slept in days.

I stood beside Karter's bike and stared. The past I had spent two decades forgetting was all too clear now. Graham had worn a helmet religiously and I never quite came to an understanding of why he wasn't wearing a helmet on the day of his accident. We had been drinking, but neither of us would have been considered drunk from a legal standpoint. Post mortem toxicology tests on Graham did indicate he had consumed alcohol, but supported the fact he was not drunk. As Graham and I had the same amount to drink, and we were the same size and weight,

KARTER

I always assumed I wasn't legally drunk either. I never really drank before the accident; and I had not one single drink of alcohol since. As Commander Warrenson always said, *men who don't drink always have a story associated with why.*

It seemed I had one too many.

We were not racing, but it was difficult for anyone to believe it. We were riding back to town on a twisting road. Both of us were knowledgeable about where we were riding and the layout of the road. As I came around the second corner, Graham shot passed me at a high rate of speed. I was traveling approximately 60 m.p.h., and I expected Graham's speed was in excess of 100 m.p.h. When I got to the fourth curve, I saw his bike in the ditch. He was against a tree beside the road, dead at the scene. His head impacted an eighty year old oak tree without a helmet to protect it. To explain the accident scene as grotesque would be an understatement.

It wasn't the first time Graham had wrecked his bike. A terrible wreck almost a month prior to his death smashed his bike up pretty bad, but his helmet saved his life. We had spent nearly two weeks solid repairing his bike prior to the second wreck, and almost immediately after the repairs, the second wreck took his life.

The damages to his motorcycle from the first accident required a repair to the exhaust port of the motor. A bolt had been pulled from the exhaust flange and out of the cast iron head during the collision, stripping the threads. A permanent heli-coil was added to repair the damaged exhaust bolt hole. At the time, it was much cheaper at ten dollars than a two thousand dollar engine. If my suspicions were correct…

After removing the bolts from the head, I pulled the exhaust to the side and pointed the flashlight in the bolt hole. Even though it was over twenty years old, the heli-coil repair we had made in my mother's garage was unmistakable. I lowered myself to the floor and pulled my knife from my pocket. On the underside of the frame in a location where it would never be detected, I began to scratch the paint from the frame. After scratching through two coats of clear coat and a few of the black away, I didn't even need my flashlight. The dark green paint was undeniable.

Karter was riding Graham's old bike.

And she had no idea of the bike's origin or who used to ride it. Two things still lingered in my mind and troubled me. I didn't need the answers immediately, but my curiosity was killing me. For one, I wanted to know why Shelley told me Karter was *my* daughter. I could see no real reason to support her making such a statement, especially when *she* knew who the father was. Secondly, I wanted to read the letters Shelley wrote. I stood in an almost trance-like state and recalled what Shelley had said prior to me asking about Karter.

"Why didn't you respond to my letters, Jak?" Shelley asked when I was preparing to leave.

"What letters?" I had responded.

I stared at Karter's bike and considered Shelley's response.

"The letters, Jak. Don't be stupid. I wrote you for a year. You never responded. Maybe once a month for a while, then I wrote once a week for a few months. I never heard from you."

I wondered what the letters may contain. I didn't need to know immediately, and they wouldn't change a thing. As far as I was concerned, Karter needed to know nothing of any of my recent findings. My secrets should remain just that, secrets. There would be zero value in Karter finding out her mother had cheated on her high school sweetheart with his best friend and became pregnant. There was a reason Shelley had never told Karter who her father was. To do so would be to admit she was a liar and a cheat. Undoubtedly, Shelley's knowledge of Graham being the father had haunted her for a lifetime. In a town of 900, to admit what she had done would cause the small city to brand her a whore and a cheat.

Regardless of who her mother may have been, I loved Karter and would always love her. I knelt down, quickly placed the two bolts back into the exhaust flange, and stood. After wiping my fingerprints from the chrome exhaust, I walked to the elevator. As I waited for the doors to open, I tossed my rubber gloves into the trash.

As the elevator reached Karter's floor, I sighed a sigh of relief.

In an almost sleep like state, I slowly stumbled to Karter's door. She was a light sleeper, and I expected she would wake up from my phone call. I scrolled to her number, pressed the icon, and listened as I heard her phone ringing through the thin walls.

"Oh my God. Jak?" she answered after two rings.

"Honey, I'm home," I sighed.

"I thought you were dead," she breathed into the phone.

"I've never been more alive," I responded, "unlock the door."

The squealing I heard from the apartment followed by the thundering steps was enough to bring me out of my sleep like state. Having no knowledge of the last four days of hell I'd been through and what I had considered, I would be far more excited by holding her than she would be by being held, that much was certain. As the door opened, I stared into the eyes of the only woman I had ever truly loved.

As she collapsed into my arms, I lifted her from the floor.

And I let her legs dangle.

JAK

"So you said we'd discuss it in the morning, it's almost ten o'clock, sleepy head, you awake yet?"

I rubbed my tired eyes and glanced toward Karter's voice. She stood beside the bed in what appeared to be a pair of jean shorts and nothing else. I blinked my eyes and tried to focus. Sure enough, she stood with paint brush in hand, half-naked and barefoot. I smiled and rolled to my side as I admired her. Karter was just...

Perfect.

"I'm awake, let me get up," I chuckled.

The house smelled of coffee and bacon. I tossed my legs to the side of the bed and pressed my feet onto the floor. As I stood, I realized I was naked. I had no real recollection of even getting into the bed the night before, let alone getting undressed. I rubbed my eyes again and looked around the room.

"On the dresser, I folded them," she grinned as she tapped the tip of the paint brush against her lip.

"I don't even remember getting undressed," I sighed as I walked to the dresser.

"You didn't. You passed out. I undressed you. I like you naked more than I like you in boxers, so..." she tilted her head to the side as I pulled my boxers over my thighs.

KARTER

"You little shit," I laughed.

She tilted her head to the other side and smiled, "So, were you on a mission?"

I turned to face her as I pulled my pants on, "Yes, and as a matter of fact, my last."

"You promise?" she asked.

I nodded my head as I buttoned my pants, "Yes, I promise."

"Were you out of the country?" she asked.

"I was in a place farther away than I have ever been," I said softly.

She shifted the weight on her feet as I approached her, bending her right knee slightly. The nipples were full on her tan perky breasts. Seeing her standing in the doorway half-naked was all I could take. To think my nightmare was over provided a relief of epic proportion.

"What did you have to do?" she asked.

"It's classified, but I can tell you this. The Commander and I had to find someone. Someone only I knew how to find. It took several days, but we found him, and everything is going to be just fine," I smiled as I reached around her and hugged her.

"Was he okay?" she asked.

I considered her question and before much thought, I responded, "No honey, he was dead. We knew he was dead; we just had to find him. But everything's fine now. That'll be the last time I ever leave you."

"I read about that. Never leave a fallen teammate behind. I like that," she breathed into my neck.

I was prepared to forget Graham, forget Shelley, forget the war, and forget the killing. It was time for me to begin my new life of loving Karter, and nothing short of doing so was going to satisfy me. As I lifted her from her feet, she squeaked and squeezed me in her arms.

"What are you working on?" I asked as I carried her out of the bedroom and toward the kitchen.

"Just goofing. Guess what?" she whispered into my ear.

"Uhhm, what?"

"I made forty grand this weekend," she said softly.

"Say again?"

"Forty. Grand," she giggled.

"How?"

"I sold everything I took to some guy in New York. He's a big time fucker of some sort. Stephen Greene. He has shiny shoes," she said matter-of-factly.

I stopped and tilted my head toward hers, "Well, good for you and good for him, I suppose. I'm proud of you, honey. But if you included the painting from my place, Stephen and I are going to have to have a little talk."

I began to step toward the kitchen with her in my arms. Having her skin against mine, in itself, reassured me Karter and I would spend forever loving each other. Now I would be able to take care of Karter, placing her wants and needs before all other things. I felt certain guilt for not being able to explain my newfound joy. To her, nothing had changed. To me, I had conquered an obstacle and opened a new door, allowing us to spend a lifetime loving each other.

Still suspended above the floor and in my arms, she bent her knees rearward and held them in place, "Nope, it's still there. I was just going to paint another. Not of me, but of you. I'm going to hang your sexy naked ass on the wall."

She kissed me on the lips lightly and I lowered her to the floor. I turned to face her easel and immediately admired an abstract likeness of my naked self on canvas. The painting wasn't quite complete, but it was clearly of me lying on my side, and from my calf to my shoulder. I changed my gaze from the painting to her and smiled without speaking.

"I took pictures of you this morning," she chuckled.

"I see," I responded, "I like it."

I turned to the kitchen counter. Three piles of mail eight inches high were stacked on the counter. Beside the mail, four newspapers sat, each opened to the obituaries. Undoubtedly she read them as soon as she returned from her weekend away. Karter and her obsessions…

"Mug the mailman?" I laughed as I nodded toward the piles of mail.

"Oh, no," she said as she stepped between me and the counter.

"I've been so preoccupied with you since we met, I hadn't been to my box. I was bored last night when I got home, so I got the mail. Ninety days' worth," she laughed.

I shook my head in disbelief. Seeing her standing in front of me half-naked and proud was a testament to who Karter was. She didn't give a shit what anyone thought. Whether or not I was in her apartment enjoying her company, she'd probably be painting naked. I softly smiled as I admired her smooth tanned skin and womanly curves. Feeling almost overwhelmed with emotion from the realization of Karter and I being able to continue our relationship, I leaned toward her and closed my eyes as we began to kiss.

As we kissed, her hand immediately reached for my belt. The anticipation of sex caused me to immediately become aroused. I kissed her more intimately until the kissing became almost rough. Together, we stumbled along the kitchen island toward the front door as we continued to kiss. She fought to unbutton my jeans. Her back slamming against the front door was a reminder we had reached the end of the corridor and ended our potential escape from what was certain to happen. I heard my zipper unzip.

"Three days is too long, Jak. I need it," she gasped as she fumbled to remove her tiny shorts.

Feeling as if I was in an entirely new and far more secure relationship with Karter, I responded differently than I expect I would have previously. I had never felt insecure with Karter or questioned our love, but now I was absolutely certain nothing could or would tear us apart.

"And I'm going to give it to you. It's a good thing you're naked, turn around," I demanded as I pressed against her left shoulder and spun her half way around.

As her body rotated, she released my jeans and they immediately fell to mid-thigh. She exhaled audibly, kicked her shorts across the floor, and leaned against the door. As she turned her head sideways and pressed her check against the wood, I raised my right foot and fought to kick my jeans to the floor. After freeing my legs from the bindings of my pants, I reached through the hole in the front of my boxers and pulled my stiff cock through it.

I reached down with both hands and gripped the bottom of her ass with my fingertips. Using my index fingers, I gently pulled her pussy lips apart, making room for my cock to slide into her with ease. Her wetness caused my fingers to slip, and as I fumbled to pull her thighs apart, she reached between her legs and guided the tip against her wetness. As I raised my fingers to meet her ass, she bent her legs and lowered herself onto me, encompassing half of my rigid shaft.

"Holy fucking shit, Jak. This feels *so good*," she gasped as she straightened her legs.

The feeling of being inside Karter wasn't one of simply having sex.

KARTER

As if the inner structure of her body was made to accept me perfectly, we carefully fit one another in a manner which was undeniable. Regardless of the position we used for our sexual adventures, everything always slid into place without pain or uncertainty. The pleasure of our bodies touching was nothing short of magic. With her face against the front door and her back arched, her ass fit against the curvature of my hips perfectly.

As she bent her legs and carefully lowered herself onto my cock, I thrust my hips upward and held them there. My upper thighs now pressed firmly against her ass, I looked down at the floor. She was standing on her tip-toes. As I focused on her feet, she lowered her heels to the floor slowly.

She struggled to turn her face away from the wooden door. As I spread my feet shoulder width apart she looked at me with sheer disgust.

With her hand between her legs, she tugged on my boxer shorts, "Are you fucking kidding me? What is this fabric matter between us, Jak?"

"I couldn't wait to take them off," I responded.

She exhaled and rolled her eyes, "That's cute Jak, but they're gross. I like looking at you when you wear them, but I don't want to fuck you with them on. Take 'em off."

I rose on the balls of my feet and pressed myself deeper into her wet pussy. She gasped, held her breath for an instant, and exhaled as she closed her eyes. Feeling as if I'd made my point, I relaxed. As I did, she arched her back drastically, pressed her hands against the door and her ass against my thighs – pulling her pussy away from my cock. As she quickly spun around and grabbed the opening of my shorts, I grinned.

She knelt in front of me and gripped the opening of my shorts. I stared down at her hair and lightly shook my head from side to side and smiled. As she looked up and met my gaze, she rolled her eyes and bit her lower lip, exposing her snow white teeth.

There was never a dull moment with Karter.

"Take," she said as she pulled against the material with both hands.

"These," she grunted as she yanked again, ripping the material slightly.

"Motherfuckers," she shouted as she tore the material even more.

"Off," with her final yank of the opening in the shorts, she tore them into two lengthwise shards of fabric. Now with an elastic waistband around my waist and two separate pieces of torn cotton dangling on either side of my upper thighs, I was free of any form of obstruction.

Sort of.

She stood from her kneeling position and stared down at the mess of material. Feeling ornery, I pressed my hands into my hips and raised one eyebrow.

"I'm not done," she breathed as she stepped around me.

I watched as she pranced to her bedroom. After a short pause, she walked from the room with her right hand clasped into a fist. As she stepped in front of me, she held her hand to her side and flicked her thumb against the blade of her knife. As it snapped into the locked position, I shook my head and chuckled.

"Don't be laughing, you might cause me to slip and slice something I don't really want to cut," she said as she slid the back side of the blade against my stomach.

With a slight upward stroke, she cut the waistband in two, and the shorts fell to the floor. I looked down at my now half flaccid cock and sighed.

KARTER

"Don't worry, baby. I'll fix that. But there's a new rule around here," she said as she nodded her head toward my waist.

Without folding the blade into the handle, she laid her knife on the edge of the kitchen countertop, "No more boxers, ever. You're going commando from here on out, agreed?"

I rolled my eyes lightly and shook my head, "Agreed."

Without a doubt, this wouldn't be the last of the changes I'd make in an effort to suit Karter. In time, we'd both be seeing differences in ourselves and in each other. For twenty years, my life had been the same thing over and over. I was prevented from making change. Now, to think I had the ability to make modifications at will and to do so with Karter's best interest in mind was extremely satisfying.

She kicked the torn pile of cotton boxers to the side and stood in front of me, smiling.

"Now maybe you won't be short stroking me," she said matter-of-factly.

As she stood naked between me and the door, I pressed my fists between my biceps and chest. I crossed my arms like an angry child and responded, "Short stroking you?"

"Mmmmhhhhm," she grinned.

"Short stroking?"

"That is affirmative sir," she nodded.

I rocked up and down on the balls of my feet, "So now I've got a little cock?"

"With that pile of shit on," she paused and pointed at the shredded shorts.

"You couldn't get *in* there. You were short stroking me. I felt like I was being fucked by a midget or something," she chuckled.

I uncrossed my arms and turned my palms upward, "A fuckin' midget?"

She raised her hand to eye level and held her thumb and forefinger two inches apart as she stared at the distance between her fingers, "Mmmhhhhm. One with a stubby little cock."

"Turn around, I'll show you just how deep I can get," I demanded.

"Promises, promises," she sighed as she slapped her hands against the door and spread her feet apart.

She looked as if she was preparing to be frisked by a police officer. My guess was she probably had a little experience at it. She looked all too versed on the procedure. Trying to act as if I was actually angry, I stroked my cock as I stepped toward her.

"You talk a lot of shit for your size," I growled.

"I'm small but I'm mean as fuck," she said over her left shoulder.

"Is that so?" I asked as I looked up and down her naked body.

With her head facing her raised left arm, and her right cheek against the door, she nodded her head slightly, "Mmmmhhhhm."

I gripped her waist in my hands and guided my half-stiff cock into her wet pussy as she arched her back and pressed her ass against me. After a few strokes, I was as hard as a rock. Now with determination and feeling as if I desperately needed to make a point, I pounded away at her pussy mercilessly.

I pressed my chin into the left side of her neck and whispered into her ear, "Feel like you're being short stroked now?"

"No," she breathed.

"Louder," I whispered.

"No!" she screamed.

The feeling of Karter's pussy around my cock was hypnotic. As if I were experiencing lovemaking for the very first time, my mind became a slave to the feeling she provided me. Even yet, I continued to breathe whispers against her ear.

"Short stroking you now, am I?" I pushed the words into her ear in short whispered bursts.

"No!" she screamed.

"With each stroke, Karter I want a yes or no, ready?" I grunted into her ear.

She bit her lower lip and nodded her head.

I pulled my hips back until the tip of my cock was touching the wet outer lips of her pussy. Slowly, I pushed my hips upward until my upper thighs lifted against her round ass. As I watched her feet lift from the floor, she grunted. As I lowered her feet to the floor, she screamed.

"No!" she screamed.

I slammed myself into her again immediately, thrusting her into the door.

"No!"

Again, I pushed my stiff cock inside of her as far as I could. With my right hand, I reached around her waist and pressed firmly against her stomach. I could feel my cock with my palm as I worked against her wet swollen pussy.

"No."

With my hand still against her stomach, I slid myself from her confines. As I stared down between the cheeks of her ass, I thrust my hips forward again, and watched my cock disappear into her wetness. As I felt the tip of my cock with my palm, I pressed harder with my right hand. Again, her feet lifted from the floor.

"No!" she screamed against the door.

"Jak, I'm..." she grunted.

Knowing she was an instant from climax, I began to fuck Karter with every ounce of my being. Pounding away without an ounce of mercy, her body slapped against the door repeatedly. As my hips slapped against her ass, my balls slapped against her clit. I pressed my chest into her back and bit her earlobe between my teeth.

"No."

"No."

"Oh fucking God. No, no, no!" she shouted as her body slapped against the door.

I felt her have repeated orgasms as she blubbered incoherently into the wall.

"Jaaaaakkkkkk," she screamed as her body went limp.

I pressed myself into her deeply and held her against the door. As she turned her head to the side, she opened her eyes slightly. Without speaking, she took a few shallow breaths and attempted to regain her composure. I kissed her deeply as I continued to feel her pussy contracting on the shaft of my cock. As her climax lessened and her breathing became normal, I slid my cock from her warm pussy.

"So?" I grinned.

"You're defo not a midget," she sighed.

"Defo?" I shrugged.

"Yep. Short for definitely. Defo. You have a big cock, Jak," she sighed as she turned around.

Her legs were shaking.

I smiled as I thought of proving my point. A sharp knock on the door startled us both. As we looked toward each other the sound came again. Four sharp knocks. I leaned toward the door and peered through the keyhole. A police officer stood on the other side of the door. I turned and looked at Karter, confused.

"It's a police officer," I whispered.

She scrunched her brow, "A cop?"

I nodded.

"Yuck. I hate cops. See what he wants," she whispered.

The officer knocked four times again.

I reached down and picked up my jeans from the floor. After pulling them on and buckling my belt, I turned toward Karter. Still standing naked in the doorway, she grinned. I pushed her to the hinge side of the door, and turned the deadbolt. As I opened the door slowly, Karter stepped between the open door and the wall, hidden from view.

The police officer looked down at my bare feet and slowly up my body, stopping his gaze even with my shoulders.

"Is everything alright?" he asked.

I nodded my head once, "Yes sir."

"We had a report of violence," he said sternly.

"A mistaken report," I said.

He leaned to the side and looked scanned the length of the hallway with his eyes. His eyes stopped where I suspected Karter laid the knife on the counter. After a short stare, he glanced at the unidentifiable pile of shredded cotton on the floor. His eyes shifted back upward and focused on mine.

"Anyone else in the house?" he asked.

I nodded my head.

Karter peered around the edge of the door, revealing her face and shoulders. I looked at the naked portion of her which was hidden by the wooden door separating her and the officer.

"Good morning, officer," she whispered.

"Ma'am, are you hurt? Are you in pain?" the officer asked.

"Not anymore," she chuckled.

"Anymore, ma'am?" the officer shifted his gaze back and forth from Karter to me repeatedly.

Karter, still hiding behind the door with only her head and shoulders exposed to the officer, turned her head upward and smiled at me. I looked down at the officer. The officer looked at Karter.

"He was fucking the shit out of me earlier, officer. And I told him he had a midget cock. You see officer, he was wearing boxers while he was trying to fuck me, and they were preventing full penetration. So, I got my *Benchmade* and cut those fuckers off. I did it for two reasons. I hated being short stroked and I don't like him wearing underwear as a general rule. He decided to teach me a lesson and fuck me even harder. We ended up against the door and maybe got carried away. All of the commotion was my face slapping the door and me screaming 'no'," she said without even smiling.

The officer tilted his head to the side, "*No*, ma'am? You were screaming no?"

"That is correct. In response to his question of whether or not he had a short cock, I responded *no* repeatedly. And my face hit the door because he was shoving me completely full of cock. He's hung like a horse, officer," she smiled as she held her index fingers a foot apart in front of the officer's face.

The officer coughed and smiled, "I see."

"So everything here is in order?" the officer asked.

I looked down between the door and the wall where Karter's body remained hidden and admired the curve of her back and her round little ass.

"Very much so," Karter nodded.

The officer nodded his head sharply, "Very well. Have a nice day."

I looked down at Karter in disbelief as I shut the door.

She grinned and stood erect as the door closed, "Well, what'd you want me to do, lie?"

I shook my head, "No, I guess not."

"Step aside, I'm hungry. Want some breakfast?" she asked as she walked between me and the door.

I watched as she walked her signature *Karter walk* into the kitchen and started digging through the pots and pans. It wasn't even noon, and Karter had painted a masterpiece, we had sex one and a half times, she cut off my underwear, we had a visit by the police, and now she was cooking brunch.

My life with Karter, if it was nothing else, would be…

Perfect.

KARTER

After Jak's last mission, he seemed to be far more willing to let himself simply exist. Almost immediately after my art show, he became more jovial, relaxed, and simple. He had never seemed uptight or robotic like I had heard other people describe former military Soldiers, Sailors, and Marines. To see him now versus seeing him before was the difference between night and day. I never would have guessed it could have been possible to enjoy him even more, but it sure was.

"I don't have my glasses, but let me see your hand, honey," his mother said as she reached for my hand.

I lifted my hand from my lap and straightened my arm to extend over the table. Gingerly, she reached under my hand with hers and lifted it to her face. As she focused on the ring she fumbled across the table with her free hand and attempted to find her glasses. After raising them to her face and pushing them onto her nose, she gasped.

"My word, that's beautiful Karter. Now when are you two thinking you'll get married?" she asked.

Jak sighed and shook his head, "Mom, we just got engaged. The marriage won't be for a while."

She looked up from the ring and over the top of her glasses toward Jak, "I wasn't talking to you, Jak. I was talking to Karter. Go in the other room if you're going to interrupt us every time we try to talk."

KARTER

"We just got here mom. If you want to call *that* an interruption, it's number one," Jak sighed.

"When would be a perfect time for you, honey? If you got to pick?" she asked.

I turned toward Jak and stared.

Help me out here, Jak.

"Don't look at him, Karter. He doesn't know a damned thing, no matter what he tries to tell you. If you got to pick, when would you want to get married? *Pay attention, Jak,*" she said as she turned her gaze toward Jak.

Lady, I like you. You make me feel good.

I looked at her and grinned. I had already thought about it. Personally, I would prefer a June wedding. It seemed like everyone did it, and although I really didn't know why, I always expected if I did get married someday, I would want to do so in June.

"I'd like a June wedding," I smiled.

"Did you hear that, Jak? She'd like a June wedding," she said as she removed her glasses and set them on the table beside her cup of coffee.

I turned my head slightly toward Jak, in hope of seeing him give confirmation of what I had said, and his acceptance of it as being okay. As always, I got exactly what I needed and wanted. His dimples showing were all the endorsement I needed. With my hand still resting in her palm, I turned to face his mother.

"Well as far as I'm concerned honey, you're already my daughter-in-law. It'll be nice to finally make it official," she said as she released my hand.

I shifted my gaze toward Jak slightly. As soon as I did, his mother snapped at me.

"Stop looking at Jak for answers, Karter. He'll do nothing but get you in trouble with those eyes of his. He'll hypnotize you with those damned things," she laughed.

I raised my hands to my cheeks, "I know, right? He does it to me all the time. He tells me things and I find myself just…"

"Go in the other room, Jak. We need to talk," his mother said softly.

"Mom, I'm not going in the other room," Jak complained.

His mother turned her head toward Jak slowly. As she reached for her cigarettes, she lowered her chin and raised her eyebrows.

"I'll be in the other room," Jak sighed.

Jak leaned over and kissed me softly. As he walked through the door and into the other room, his mother stood from her chair, tip-toed to the doorway, and stared into the other room. After a silent moment of her staring into the living room, she turned around and walked to the table and sat down.

"You've got to keep an eye on him, he's a sneaky one. We don't need him listening to our girl talk," she said as she scooted her chair closer to the table.

"Now we can talk," she smiled.

I grinned and nodded my head, "Okay."

"I want this to work for all of us, honey. You and Jak. So, I'm going to give you what little advice I can," she said as she lit a cigarette.

As she began to smoke her cigarette, she looked around the kitchen as if she was thinking of what to say next. Silently, she continued to smoke and look down at the ashtray. I sat nervously and waited for her to continue. After a few moments of her not speaking, I decided to say *something*.

"We'll be just fine, I'm sure of it. We don't fight or argue at all. I really think he loves me as much as I love him. And I love him more than I can ever sit here and try to explain," I said.

She looked up from the ashtray, "I'm sure you do. He's told me over and over how much he loves you - 'till he's blue in the face. I'm happy for us all. I don't have much experience, Karter. Not with men. Jak's father died when he was a little boy. I never remarried or even saw another man after his father was gone. I couldn't bring myself to. It wouldn't have been fair to either of us. I still loved Jak's father then and I still love him today."

"What was his name? Jak's father?" I asked.

"His name was Anderson. Jak didn't tell you? His name was Anderson Jackson Kennedy. We named Jak so his initials would spell his name. We thought it was cute. Jak Anderson Kennedy. J.A.K.," she smiled.

I smiled and nodded. For some reason, I preferred having names attached to people in the tales which were told about them. Without a name, the story meant less and it was difficult to believe. Simply having a name made everything become real. Without one, the statements felt meaningless and weak. As she puffed on her cigarette she looked at me as if she wanted to eat me.

She smiled and tilted her head back as she blew smoke in the air, "Karter, you're a beautiful woman. I like looking at your face, it's beautiful. You remind me of a girl I went to school with. Her name was Jennifer. She was the prettiest girl in school. I envied her. I wanted to be as pretty as her, but it never worked out that way. You're prettier than she was, and she has always been the prettiest girl I've ever known. You just shoved her aside and took over."

You make me feel so good. I can't wait to have you as a mother.

You're adorable.

"Thank you very much. That's nice of you to say. I liked hearing it. You're adorable," I smiled.

She grinned and smashed her cigarette into the ashtray, "Okay so there's a few things I want to tell you. You may already know, but if you do, just entertain me. I want to feel like you learned them from me. Okay, honey?"

I nodded my head and smiled.

"Now, you and Jak. At some point in time, you will have a disagreement. It's bound to happen. When it does, make sure you get it resolved before bedtime. Never go to sleep angry with the one you love," she picked up her cigarette case, looked inside and closed the case.

"And, when you have a disagreement, never raise your voice. It's hard for a man to scream at a woman if she's whispering. So, if you're arguing, keep it quiet and make whatever point you have to without raising your voice. Loud doesn't make right."

I couldn't imagine Jak screaming at me, but her advice made perfect sense. It was nice to have someone care enough to sit and talk about their relationship opinions and give advice. It would be far too easy for me to spend a few days a week with Jak's mother talking about things I've never felt comfortable talking to other people about. She seemed to spend most of her time at home, and almost all of it in the kitchen, but she spent it alone. As I sat and admired her for being so sweet, I felt terrible for her being alone for the last twenty years.

"And when it comes to sleeping, before you go to sleep tell Jak you love him. Do it every night. And give him a kiss. Do it in bed, not a half hour before or anything silly. And every morning when you wake up, kiss him and tell him you love him before you get out of bed. You'll reach a point when you'll feel like he knows, but tell him anyway. It's always nice to say and it's sure nice to hear."

She reached across the table toward my hands. Without thought, I straightened my arms and extended my hands toward hers. Our fingers met in the middle of the table. As she held my hands softly in hers, she looked up into my eyes and smiled.

"I love you, Karter."

If you make me cry, I'm going to throat punch you.

I wanted to tell her I loved her too. I wished I knew her name. As if she knew what prevented me from immediately responding, she spoke.

"Jaqueline. You can call me Jackie," she said softly.

And at that particular moment, everything she had said became real. I felt warm inside. As I held her hands in mine, I swallowed and responded without any thought.

"I love you too, Jackie."

JAK

"Jak, you's one lyin' ass motherfucker. 'Scuse the language Miss Karter. Jak told me you was pretty. What he went on and failed to tell me was that you defined the word. Lord have mercy woman, you make everything around you ugly as a motherfucker," Oscar said as he walked across the shop floor.

Oscar was simply Oscar. He had his way of speaking, thinking, and of telling his stories. After repeated requests to meet Karter, I finally decided to bring her to the school and introduce her to him. School had started and was in session, so I hadn't been coming to the track to run any longer. My trips to see Oscar, however, never ceased.

Karter cocked her hip to the side as if offended, "What do you mean?"

Oscar stopped directly in front of her an extended his hand. Karter reluctantly reached for his. As they shook hands, Oscar explained.

"Well, look around you, Miss Karter. You see Jak's ugly ass and me. Some old black man. I got my golf cart, and a bunch a broken ass shit in here. We gots a few trees out the door over there, and some grass. That's about all we got. A little blue sky if you take the time to look up. But when *you* walk into a room," he paused and released her hand.

"Whoooooeeeeeee. Things change. You's so God damned beautiful, you make everything else what seemed kinda pretty before you arrived look about as ugly as a mud fence in your presence. I don't rightly know how else to tell ya. But you uhhm. You, how you say it, Jak?" he paused and raised his hand to his chin.

"You redefine the word, Miss Karter. That's the one I was lookin' for. *Redefine.* You redefine beautiful," he nodded.

Karter smiled and shook her head. As if she finally understood what Oscar had said wasn't an insult, she sighed and her shoulders slumped slightly, "You're not ugly, and neither is Jak. Pleasure to meet you, Oscar."

"We's a damned site uglier with you around. Hold on I gots to get me somethin' from my bench," he said as he turned toward the workbench.

After a moment of digging, Oscar turned around. He was wearing welding goggles. The goggles he wore looked like World War II era fighter pilot goggles with black hinged outer lenses. The outer lenses were flipped in the upward position, exposing the inner clear lenses. After walking to his former position in front of Karter, he flipped down the black lenses and looked downward. Having welded in the Navy, I knew Oscar could not see a damned thing with the welding goggles on. Without the bright flash of a welding arc, the lenses would be like attempting to look through a piece of glass which had been painted black. I thought I knew what he was going to say, but I kept my mouth shut. Karter seemed amused if nothing else.

"Sorry, Miss Karter. I had to go an' get my goggles on so I could look at the ring. Damned thing almost made me blind. She's a dandy, Miss Karter," as he finished speaking, he whistled.

Oscar looked upward and flipped the outer lenses up as he did. Now standing in front of Karter with the goggles still on, he smiled. His bleach white teeth were in clear contrast to everything about him.

He was one of a kind for sure. Karter looked around the shop as Oscar turned toward me and winked.

"So what do you do in here all day?" Karter asked.

"Hide from the man and try an' look busy," he grinned.

Karter nodded her head, "Who's *the man*?"

"Well I suppose he's different for all of us. For me, he's the school superintendent. Least while I'm here. Sometimes the man is the police. Or the gov'ment. Could be the president, I suppose. But right now, he's the superintendent," he responded.

With Karter and Oscar standing in the center of the small shop, I slowly walked to the golf cart and sat down to watch the show. It appeared Karter was becoming comfortable with Oscar and enjoyed listening to him. He was an easy man to like, and fairly entertaining to listen to.

Karter nodded her head, "Whoever's in charge."

Oscar shook his head, "No ma'am. I don't mind a man in charge. Hell, we all can't be the boss man. We'd have us a fucked up world with a bunch of Chiefs and no Indians. No ma'am. But if a man's in charge, and he's always tryin' to keep the people around him down, and never smiles at 'em or never tells 'em they's doin' good; if he tries to beat 'em down mentally or 'motionally then he's *the man*."

Karter pushed her hands into the rear pockets of her jeans shorts, swiveled her hips, and smiled, "People with mustaches."

Oscar reached up and removed his goggles. As they dangled from his hand, he scrunched his brow, "You got me there, Miss Karter. What you mean by that?"

"People with mustaches are *the man*. The Unabomber. Stalin. Saddam Hussein. Hitler. And most cops," she giggled.

KARTER

Oscar erupted with laughter and turned to face me, "Jak this girl's on fire. Damn, I like you, Miss Karter. *People with mustaches.* Yes ma'am, they's the man fo' sho'."

Oscar slapped his knee, "Mustaches. That crazy ass white boy what was eatin' them gays. You remember, Jak? He was cuttin' 'em up and keepin 'em in the freezer. He had a mustache. Was uhhm…"

"Dahmer. Jeffrey Dahmer. He had a mustache. And so did that Mo…" he turned to face me and grinned.

"Ol' Gaddafi. From Libya. He had him one too. Miss Karter, you's right as rain. Men with mustaches is *the man*," he laughed.

As if satisfied she made a friend, Karter rocked back and forth on her feet with her hands still resting in her rear pockets. Seeing her stand in this fashion made me recall the day we talked about sex for the first time. No differently than the rest of us, she had her tell-tale signs. This was certainly one of them. She did it when she wanted to make herself comfortable with something she initially found not so comfortable. Whatever the reason, she was adorable when she did it.

"So when's the date? When you gettin' hitched?" Oscar asked.

Karter shrugged and smiled, "Sometime in June."

"Be here before you know it, that's fo' sho'. Weddin's and anniversaries. They's always creepin' up on us. Well, Jak's a good man, Miss Karter. Sho' 'nuff is. I don't like me too many white folk, an' I like him just fine," he chuckled.

"He's pretty fly for a white guy," Karter laughed.

We stayed and talked in the shop for over an hour. Karter and Oscar laughed and told stories together as I sat on the golf cart and listened. Seeing her interact with Oscar was a pleasure in itself. I found satisfaction in thinking of us returning on a regular basis. Developing routines was important for me, and having one as enjoyable as visiting with Oscar would be a welcome addition to our schedule.

"Oscar, I'll need to see you in my office as soon as you're done visiting," a voice said from outside the shop door.

"Yes sir, Mr. James, sir. Be in to see you in just a few minutes," Oscar responded.

I stood from the golf cart feeling guilty for occupying so much of Oscar's time. As I walked around the front of the cart, Karter broke out in a deep laughter. Oscar raised his hand in Jonny Cash fashion and flipped the bird at the open door.

"What's so funny?" I asked.

After a moment of attempting to catch her breath, Karter turned to me and smiled, "He had a mustache."

Oscar furrowed his brow and turned to Karter, "I never noticed. He does, don't he?"

Karter nodded as she caught her breath from laughing, "Uh huh."

"I gots to get to work now. You like hugs, Miss Karter?" Oscar asked.

"Only if you leave my feet on the ground," Karter replied.

"Well give this old black man a hug," Oscar said as he opened his arms.

As Oscar hugged Karter, he closed his eyes. Her feet firm on the floor, Karter turned to me and winked. As Oscar released her, she walked up to me and spread her arms apart. I hugged her in my arms, arched my back, and raised her feet from the floor. Still holding her in my arms, I stumbled toward the doorway.

"Thanks, Oscar. I'll be seeing you," I said as I carried Karter through the doorway.

"Not if I see you first," he laughed.

JAK

I tossed the lid to the chest up and looked inside. Several bundles of letters were stacked inside. With my old photo album sitting beside the chest, I knelt down and sorted through the bundles. Looking at the faded post marks on the envelopes, I sorted them on the floor beside me by date. After Fifteen minutes or so, I had all of the bundles in chronological order. A few loose letters and other miscellaneous keepsakes littered the bottom of the almost empty chest.

I picked up the first bundle and untied the stack of envelopes. After flipping through a few, I found one from Shelley. I flicked my knife open and cut the twenty year old envelope and removed the letter. Surprisingly, although the pencil handwriting was a little faded, the paper wasn't brittle at all. After unfolding it, I took a deep breath and began to read.

Jak,

I feel terrible and would like to talk. The last few days before you left were difficult for me. I have so much to say. I really need to talk to you about some things. I hope your training goes well, and you make it to the end. I know it will be tough and if anyone can do it, you can.

Looking forward to hearing from you.

Shell

I folded the letter and placed it back into the envelope. I picked up the pile and turned the corners of the envelopes up, looking at the return addresses as I did so. After finding another from Shelley, I opened it and removed the letter.

Jak,

I still haven't heard back from you, but I have no idea how long the letters take to reach you. The weather is shitty here, and it snowed a lot last week. We're all kind of stuck here, and waiting for it to melt. It reminds me of the time we went sledding down at the river when we were kids.

I miss everyone being together.

We really need to talk. Write when you can. I asked, and I can't send food, or I would. Hope you're eating well. Keep your chin up.

Shell

I folded the letter and placed it back into the envelope. There were certainly no earth shattering revelations as I had hoped. I looked at the various piles of letters, and considered when Karter would have been born. I picked up a pile of letters dated approximately six months after I had shipped out and untied the bundle. After a few letters, I found one from Shelley. I cut it open and removed the letter.

Jak,

I can't believe you still haven't written. If you're mad because I won't tell you who the father is, I guess you have the right to be. I would have thought in some sense the fact it wasn't you would allow you a little relief. If you would have written or if you'll still write, maybe we can talk about it. Maybe one day I will tell you.

I'm doing fine, I guess. I'm really big and everyone is confused. Same old shit, I suppose. Hope you're well.

Shell

I folded the letter and dropped it into the envelope. Satisfied I'd never get to anything meaningful, and having read her acknowledgement of me *not* being the father was enough. Although I wanted answers, I began to realize they would not be provided. I had held onto the memories of my childhood for a lifetime, and the time had clearly arrived for me to let go and move on with my life. Things were beginning to be so much different in now. After seeing Shelley, finding out who Karter's father was and slowly coming to terms with it all, I felt relieved and considerably less responsible for everything. In time, I was sure I'd probably just forget it all and move on a much better man.

I looked at the pile and considered what to do with it all. By no means did I want Karter to ever find it. In many respects, I wished none of it even existed. As I sat and stared at the piles of old mail, I decided it would never be of any future use. I looked into the chest. As I began to rummage through the remaining contents, one lone letter caught my eye.

My heart raced. I picked it up and stared at the return address.

Graham Lauder 329 N 9th, Potwin, KS 67123

I blinked my eyes and stared at the faded postmark date.

18 JAN 1993

Believing I must be misreading the date, I stood from the floor and walked to the lamp in the corner of the room. I blew on the surface of the envelope and wiped the date with the bottom of my tee shirt. I stared at the envelope. It was as if it was shipped from a ghost.

18 JAN 1993

Graham was killed on the 14th of January. I shipped out on the night of the 21st. I considered the date he was killed and tried to recall the day of the week. It was an extremely warm day in mid-January, and we decided to go for another ride because of the fabulous weather. The forecast had called for three sixty-five degree days back to back. We had worked eagerly to bring his bike to a condition where he could ride it, and waited anxiously to for the nice weather. The day he died was a Wednesday. No, it was a Thursday. Thursday the 14th.

The letter postmarked the 18th clearly meant one thing and one thing only. Graham had mailed it to me before he died. If he would have mailed it from Potwin on the morning he died, the postmark would probably be correct. Mail was taken from Potwin to Wichita for a postmark, and then distributed from Wichita to the respective destination. The cycle, considering the weekend, could have been a week. My mother had probably simply dropped it into the chest and left it with the other mail I had sent home.

Reluctantly, I walked to the chest and picked my knife up from the floor. As I cut the envelope open and removed the letter, I sighed. After slowly unfolding it, I began to read.

Jak,

I don't know how to say it other than saying it, so here goes.

I'm probably dead or in a coma. I told myself if I lived through this one I'd make it to your mailbox and get the letter out like I did last time. If you're reading this, it ain't gonna be good.

I couldn't believe what I was reading. I blinked my watering eyes and continued.

When we go riding, I won't be wearing my helmet this time. I won't be going to basic training with you either. I got Shelley pregnant back in October last year, and she wants to get married. It's tough to tell you she's a bad person, because I'm just as bad. But she's no good, Jak. She's been fucking around on you for most of the time you two have been together. I been trying to think of a way to tell you, but I couldn't bring myself to. I guess really I don't know if I'm the father, but I can't wait and see. I can't go to the Navy with you and wait to see what happens, it's a huge mess, Jak.

My tears fell onto the letter as I read. I wiped my eyes with the back of my hand and lowered the letter. My entire life I took responsibility for what had happened to Graham. The feelings were so deeply placed in my soul, my mind eventually had to block them out to allow me to continue to live a healthy life.

But I lived feeling responsible for what happened. I always wondered if we hadn't been drinking if things may have gone differently. It wouldn't have mattered. Graham was on his second suicide mission. I looked down at the letter. Slowly, I raised it to chest height and began to read again.

I can't live my life with an all day every day reminder of what a bad friend I was, and I ain't looking to raise a kid with a whore (sorry, but it's true). So I guess I'm going to go out with a bang. I'm sorry for what I did, and I'm sorry for what I'm going to do. I hope you understand.

I just hurt really bad inside.

I left mom and pop a letter telling them bye. I ain't telling them about Shelley, and I hope you don't either. After the kid's born if he looks like me I'll guess we'll know.

I love ya, Jak. And I'm really sorry.
Graham

I reread the entire letter. After folding it and placing it into the envelope, I gathered all of the mail and dropped it into the wooden box. I tossed the photo album on top and closed the lid to the chest. I pushed my knife into my pocket and clipped it in place. After a precursory look around the room, I carried the heavy chest to the top of the steps.

The drive to Potwin seemed to take mere minutes. As close as I could recall, I was exactly where Graham had wrecked his bike. In lieu of going to his grave site, I opted to drive to the crash site. For me, it seemed more reasonable and personal. After all, it was where Graham took his last breath. In my mind, this was where he would always remain. I pulled my truck partially into the ditch and parked.

I walked back to the bed of the truck and opened the chest. After lifting out the photo album, I carried it back to the cab of the truck. I opened the album and removed Graham's picture from the translucent film which covered it. His appearance in the photo was exactly as I remembered him. I smiled and placed the photo on the dash. After resting the album on my lap, I turned the picture over and began to write on the back of it. This was important; I needed to let him go and move on with my life.

Graham,

I forgive you for what you did. I still and I will always consider you a friend. I'm going to spend a lifetime taking care of your daughter, but not because she's your daughter. She'll forever be in my life only because I love her and I can't imagine living a life without her.

To think somehow I happened onto her and we fell in love - and all of this isn't tied together somehow would require me to be a very shallow man. We both know that is not the case. God put Karter in my life for me to love and cherish, and I intend to do so with great vigor. This will be the last time you and I will ever talk, so I'll leave you with these words:

The events in life we can't accept are always the toughest.

And the toughest events in life are always the ones we can't accept.

I think when we can find a way to heal from pieces of the very things which have torn us apart, we truly emerge a better person.

So, I'm going to buy a bike. And I'm going to ride that son-of-a-bitch until the day I die.

Your friend always,

Jak

I turned the photo over and placed it into the album. After a short pause, I opened the door to the truck and walked around to the rear bumper. I looked in the bed of the truck at the can of gasoline and grinned. Moving forward would be a blessing for us all. I tossed the album into the chest, lifted it from the bed, and carried it to the base of the old tree.

As I sat on the bed of the truck and watched my memories burn, I realized there was not one person in charge of my destiny but me. The only thing which separated me from a life of greatness was me. I was a great Navy SEAL. I've always considered myself a great son. Now, it was time for me to become a great lover and a great husband.

One more stop, and my past would truly be behind me.

After a short ten minute drive, I arrived at Shelley's house. This time I pulled my truck into the driveway. After a deep breath, I walked to the porch and rang the doorbell. After no immediate answer, I knocked on the door and stepped to the side. As it opened, Shelley smiled.

"Come on in, Jak," she said softly as she waved her hand into the living room.

"No, I just have a few things to say, and I'll be gone," I responded.

"Why'd you do it, Shelley? Why'd you tell me Karter was mine when you knew she wasn't?" I asked.

KARTER

"How do you know she's not?"

"I had a DNA test done," I responded.

Although part of me wanted to, I felt no good would come from her knowing Graham committed suicide. As far I knew, she received a letter no differently than I did. It could have been why she'd lived a miserable existence for the last twenty years. Additionally, I felt no need to tell her I knew who the father was; only that I knew for certain who the father was not.

"Oh really? Well…" she paused and looked down at my feet.

I nodded and waited in hope of her explaining herself.

She looked up and narrowed her eyes, "Pete said he ran into you guys in town, I saw him the morning you came over. I saw him at the gas station and he said he'd seen the both of you in Wichita at a fancy restaurant. He said it looked like you were together. Like *together*, Jak. It hurt me. And I wanted you to hurt. I was going to tell you when you were here, and then you asked. It just seemed right lying to you about it. Are you fucking her, Jak?"

I stood and stared. After a long moment of studying her hateful eyes, I shook my head and turned toward my truck. As I walked to the truck, she began to scream.

"I hate that little miserable bitch, Jak. I always have. She's got a heart of stone and so do you. I wish they would have committed her the last time I turned her filthy little ass in to the court for being crazy. I hate you both and I hope you rot in hell," she yelled.

As I got into the truck, I continued to hear her scream.

"I hate you, Jak Kennedy…"

"Go to hell!"

Hell? I've lived there for twenty-one years.

SCOTT HILDRETH

I'm upgrading to heaven, bitch.
Starting now.

KARTER

"It's the cable that goes between the battery and the starter. It's got an eyelet on each end, one for the battery post and one for the bolt in the starter."

"What year?" he asked.

Are you fucking kidding me? We've been over this already.

I slapped my hands onto the edge of the counter. I glanced over my shoulder. Jak was wandering the showroom floor looking at the various bikes on display. I bit my lip and tried to keep from making a fool of myself by screaming at the eighteen year old incompetent parts salesman. I looked down at his Harley-Davidson logo tattoo on his forearm and his well-manicured fingernails. No doubt he'd never worked on his own Harley, if he even had a Harley.

"1991. Softail. Evo. 1340 cc. Battery cable from the battery to the starter," I sighed.

He looked at the computer screen and tapped aimlessly at the keys on the keyboard. After a few moments, and without speaking, he turned and walked to the door which led to the warehouse. I stared down at my left hand and contemplated getting knuckle tattoos as I waited for him to return. As I admired my ring in the bright lighting of the store, he returned with a plastic baggy. As he tossed it on the counter, I looked down at the clear plastic wrapper. My initial relief was quickly overcome by anger as I noticed the twelve inch long black cable.

"What the fuck is that?" I asked as I nodded toward the baggie, "Someone else's shit?"

"Battery cable," he said flatly.

"Battery cable for what?" I asked as I raised the baggie in the air for him to see.

"1991 Softail Evo," he responded.

You fucking idiot.

"Positive or negative?" I asked.

"Positive."

I took a deep breath. As much as I didn't want to make a scene, my voice quickly elevated as I began to speak, "What fucking color is positive? On a car, boat, bike, or even a fucking snowmobile?"

He shrugged, "Red?"

I shook my head, "That's fucking right. Red. Now *dumbass*, what color is this?"

I raised the baggie in the air for him to see the black cable inside. Clearly it was the negative cable, and it was at least a foot too short to reach my starter.

"Black?"

I nodded my head, "It sure as fuck is. It's black. Did you even look at this motherfucker before you tossed it in front of me?"

"Hey, you don't have to talk to me like this," he whined.

I pressed my hands into my back pockets, "You know what, you're right. In fact, I don't have to talk to you at all. Go get Kelli. I want to talk to her."

He rolled his eyes and picked up the baggie.

"I'm serious. Get Kelli," I demanded.

He turned toward the door leading into the warehouse. As he began to walk away, I tilted my head back and looked up at the structure of the ceiling.

"Kelli!" My voice echoed through the showroom as I screamed.

As I stood at the parts counter waiting, I turned toward the showroom floor. Jak stood talking to one of the sales staff beside a new Harley bagger. As our eyes met he smiled, undoubtedly about my having screamed. By now he had to know I was a very vocal person. In turning back toward the counter, I heard Kelli's very familiar voice.

"Karter!" I heard her screech as she stepped out of her office and into the customer area.

"You're *always* in here. What are you doing?" she asked as she leaned into me and hugged me lightly.

One thing about owning a Harley is the fact they always need worked on. Sooner or later, they'll break down and need repairs. Harley aficionados know the value in using Harley-Davidson parts on their Harley's. And the only place to go get original Harley parts is at the Harley dealer. Wichita had only one Harley dealer, and although it used to be run by a bunch of shit-heads, Kelli's father bought the dealer and gave it to her and her husband. After they took over, things changed drastically. The dealer was now run by bikers who rode, knew Harley's in and out, and were all around good people. Kelli was the president and owner. She and I got along from the day we first met.

"I'm always in here because my shit's always broke down," I smiled and paused, "who's this dumb fuck parts kid? What is he, sixteen?"

Kelli shook her head, "He's Derek's nephew."

"The Bone?" I asked.

Kelli nodded her head.

KARTER

"Well he's a good solid guy, but his nephew's a fucking idiot. I need a starter cable and he brought me a negative ground cable. Where's Teddy or Jake?" I asked.

She looked down at her watch, "Teddy should be back in like ten minutes."

"I don't know where the dumb fuck kid went. I'll just wait for my man Teddy," I grinned.

Teddy was as big as Jak plus thirty pounds. He had a full beard, arms as big as my legs, and a massive chest. He was built like an old school pro wrestler and was as nice as anyone I'd ever met. He had a gravelly voice and talked in almost a southern slang. Seeing him was always a pleasure of mine when I came in and he helped me. Having him assist me instead of the incompetent piece of shit who was trying would possibly make my day a little more enjoyable. Teddy always had at least one story to tell, and they were always funny.

"Okay. Well, it was nice seeing you, Karter," Kelli smiled.

"Same to ya," I grinned.

Kelli was beautiful and had jet black hair. She was tiny and very quiet. She married another member of the club who everyone said used to be a doctor. He didn't look like a doctor, he looked like a biker. I'd seen him around, and at a few poker runs, as their club had a tremendous presence at all of the local poker runs. He seemed nice, and he was good to Kelli, but I didn't personally trust him. Something about him just seemed off. My guess was that he was mean in private and nice in public. I guessed as long as Kelli was happy with him that was all that mattered. I turned from the counter and walked toward where Jak stood.

"Karter, I want you to meet Steve. His dad was a SEAL. He died about the time I went into the Navy," Jak said as soon as I approached.

"Steve, this is my fiancé, Karter," Jak smiled as he pointed to the salesman.

"Nice to meet you. Sorry about your father," I nodded.

The salesman nodded in return and shook my hand, "I've seen you around a few times. I'm not here much, only in shitty weather and in the winter. You're hard to miss with all the tats."

"Yeah, the tats and the 'tude," I laughed.

"You found Kelli?" he asked.

I nodded, "I'm waiting on Teddy to get back from lunch."

I turned from the salesman to Jak, "You mind waiting for another fifteen minutes?"

Jak shook his head, "No. as a matter of fact, I was thinking about riding this bike."

"Say again?" I chuckled.

I couldn't believe my ears. Before he had a chance to respond, I excitedly blurted out another question, "Why?"

The thought of being able to ride with Jak was beyond exciting to me. I had purchased the motorcycle from my mother when I was fifteen. It had been in her garage as long as I could remember. She had told me she got a really good deal on it when I was a kid, and had kept it in hopes of someday having a boy. She never had another child, and when I turned fifteen I bought it for five hundred bucks. I studied on the internet, read repair manuals, and repaired it myself. Two summers later, I had the awful green paint job repainted to black. I'd never ridden with anyone else, but always wanted to. The thought of being able to share something I held as sacred as riding excited me to no end. Hell, I'd even teach him to ride.

"Well, I thought we could ride together," he shrugged.

KARTER

"Fuck yeah we can," I squealed.

I glanced back and forth between the salesman and Jak. It was so exciting to think of Jak on a bike. I wanted him to hop on it, ride it, and buy it. I leaned between Jak and the salesman and wrapped my arms around Jak. As he hugged me, I raised my mouth to his ear.

"I thought you hated bikes. Do you know how to ride?" I whispered.

He nodded his head, "I used to ride. I always loved it," he whispered in return.

You cocksucker, I can't believe you kept this from me.

"Seriously?" I said softly.

He nodded his head and kissed me lightly.

"I'll be right back, I'm going to grab the keys," Steve said.

"Alright," Jak responded as he released me.

"You fucker. You ride?" I gasped.

"I used to. I had a friend who was killed on one, so I stopped. I just came to the realization it wasn't anyone's fault but his. He'd been drinking and he was speeding," he said softly.

"I'm sorry about your friend, but you're right. Alcohol and bikes," I paused and shook my head, "that's a bad mix."

"Sure is," he responded.

"So, seriously, you're going to ride it?"

He nodded his head eagerly.

Holy fuck. Jak on a bike.

I looked at the black Street Glide. It was gorgeous. Thinking of riding together began to excite me greatly. Riding on the back of Jak's bagger would be a blast. The thought of holding on to him with the wind in our faces and Jak wearing a wife beater and his boots...

Rollin' sex.

"Karter, you little fucker," I heard Teddy scream across the showroom floor.

I turned to toward the parts department. Teddy stood on the other side of the counter waving his arms like an idiot. I turned to face Jak and grinned.

Shit, I'm soaked.

"Shit, Jak," I sighed.

"Is there a problem?" he asked.

"Not with him, no. That's Teddy, he's cool. The problem," I paused, looked down at my crotch, and nodded my head once.

Jak looked down at the floor and slowly up and into my eyes. His eyes widened and he raised his eyebrows in wonder.

"My pussy," I sighed.

"Oh, did you start your period?" he whispered.

"No I didn't start my period, dork. Thinking about you on a bike made me wet. Stick your hand in here," I said as I pulled the waist of my jeans away from my stomach.

Jak looked around the dealership and down at the waist of my jeans.

Oh fuck yes, I was totally kidding, but do it.

Do it.

Stick your hand in my pants.

"I can't. Not in here," he whispered.

You big pussy.

I shook my head and released the waist of my jeans. I raised my index finger between us and used my smart assed voice, "You might be big, and you might buy a bike, but you've got a ways to go to be *a biker*."

That ought to do it.

KARTER

In some instantaneous SEAL judo move, he snatched me from my feet and tossed me to the side and onto the seat of the bike he was looking at. My ass landed perfectly onto the oversized leather seat. As he held me by the front of my shirt with one hand, he stuck his other hand into the front of my pants. I leaned back into the seat, closed my eyes, and arched my back. As he slid his finger into my pussy, I shivered and almost knocked the bike over.

He pressed his finger deep into me and curled it upward.

Oh God, my g-spot.

He pressed it even deeper and curled the tip of his finger into my g-spot again. I opened my eyes, stared up at him, and bit my lip.

One more of those, and I'll cum.

"One more," I whispered.

He shook his head and smiled. Slowly, he pulled his hand from my pants and raised his soaked finger to his mouth. As his lips parted, he closed his eyes.

Do it, fuck yes. That's fucking hot.

He slid his pussy soaked finger into his mouth and sucked on it.

"You're a dick," I said as I stood from the seat.

He smiled and nodded, "I can be."

"I almost came," I sighed.

He grinned, "I know. You're weak, Karter."

"Weak for you. *I hate you,*" I whispered jokingly and I rearranged my jeans.

"Karter!" Teddy screamed.

"I better go get my cable," I sighed.

"Looks like it," Jak chuckled.

"Be right back," I smiled as I turned toward the parts department.

Teddy stood beside the counter with his forearms leaning on the outer edge of the top. His arms were as big if not bigger than my legs, and his forearms were equally as large. As I walked up to the counter, he raised his right hand, opened it, and flattened his palm. I did the same with mine and slapped his open hand. Immediately, he made a fist. I did the same and pounded mine against his.

Every time he greeted me, it was with the same handshake.

"Little Karter. How's that Evo?" he growled.

"Be better if I had a positive cable for it. Battery to starter," I responded.

"1991?" he asked.

"Good memory," I nodded.

"Well, it's pretty fuckin' easy. You're the only tattooed supermodel who rides an Evo Softail. Be right back," he said as he turned toward the warehouse.

After sixty seconds, Teddy walked form the back room with a cable in his hand. From what I could see, it was the correct cable.

Fuck yes.

"This fucker was back there without a baggie. Looks right to me," he winked.

"How much?" I asked as I reached for my wallet.

"Can't rightly charge for it. It ain't got a fuckin' part number," he shrugged, "I don't even know how to put it in the computer."

I shook my head and smiled. Teddy leaned onto the counter and looked to his left and then to his right. As he stopped looking around and focused on me, he grinned.

"Wanna hear a story?" he asked.

I nodded eagerly, leaned onto the counter, and shoved the battery

KARTER

cable into my pocket.

"You know Kelli, right?" he tilted his head toward Kelli's office.

I nodded and smiled.

"She's fuckin' preggo," he smiled.

"Huh? I just saw her a minute ago. She didn't look it," I shrugged.

"Well, she's preggo as a motherfucker. Doc knocked her up on a bet," he leaned back and slapped the countertop with his open hand.

"On a bet?"

He nodded his head and leaned into the counter again, "Yep. Went to a boxing match in Texas. Doc says, *if this sum bitch knocks out the Alabama boy, I'll give ya a baby*. So, the kid knocks out the Alabama boy. And Kelli tosses the birth control in the shit-can. About three weeks, and she's fuckin' preggo."

He raised his hand and snapped his fingers loudly, "Just like that."

I smiled, "Well, good for her. I'll congratulate her on the way out."

Having a baby with Jak would be the best gift I could ever receive. To think of Jak and me raising a child together made me think of the differences between what my mother did and what I would do. My child, if I was ever so lucky to have one, would receive nothing but love and affection. I know Jak well enough to know he'd provide the exact same thing. For a small moment as I stood there, I became jealous of Kelli for being pregnant and me not even being married yet.

"Wait, that ain't the half of it," he said as he leaned away from the counter and rubbed his hands together.

I raised my eyebrows in false wonder, "Oh it isn't?"

"Nope. Guess?" he said as he began to rub his beard.

I shrugged, "Uhhm. I don't know. Twins?"

"Sum bitch. You guessed it. Damn, you're good, Karter," he

chuckled.

"Seriously? Twins?" I asked.

"Yep. Boy and a girl. They got one a them whatchamacallit tests. And there's one a each in there," he grinned.

I pressed my tongue to the roof of my mouth and wrinkled my nose, "That might be a little tough, going from none to two immediately."

Teddy shrugged and smiled. All of a sudden I wasn't so jealous. To think of having two kids at once seemed like more of a hassle than a blessing. Maybe if they were my kids, I'd feel differently. I smiled at the overall thought of children and of Kelli probably being excited about having twins.

"Is that it?" I asked.

"Well," he rubbed his beard again with both hands.

"Oh, shit. I almost forgot," I said as I lifted my left hand to the counter.

"Bam!" I shouted as my hand hit the counter.

Teddy jumped backward as if I had actually scared him. As he looked down at my hand, his eyes widened and he grinned.

"Sum bitch girl. From him? The big boy?" he nodded his head toward the showroom.

I smiled, "Yep. I'll introduce you. He's thinking about buying the Street Glide."

"He better buy it," Teddy said as he leaned away from the counter.

"Oh yeah? Why so?"

As he slowly walked toward the back room, he looked over his left shoulder and chuckled, "If you finger bang a girl on one of our bikes, you gotta buy it."

And with that, Teddy disappeared into the back room. I turned toward the showroom and noticed Jak was gone. I looked toward the front door. Steve and Jak were pushing the bike through the open doors. Excitedly, I ran toward the door. As I caught up to them, they were pushing the bike onto the sidewalk.

"So, you going to ride it?" I asked.

"Yes, I am. Let me get my feet wet for a few minutes, it's been a while. I'll be back in about ten," he grinned.

The bike looked gorgeous in the sunlight. The thought of mine being broke down made me more disappointed now, as Jak and I couldn't ride together until I fixed it. As Steve stepped to the side, Jak pulled a half-helmet on and fired up the bike. As the engine warmed, he turned toward me and tilted his head to the side.

"Kiss me," he said.

I wrapped my arms around him and gave him a kiss. Seeing him on the bike excited me to no end. As I stepped on the sidewalk and watched, Jak pulled out onto the road in front of the dealership and gassed the throttle like he was in a street race. I smiled as he sped away and up the onramp to the highway.

"Ridin' that motherfucker like he stole it," Steve laughed.

"Well, at least he isn't riding it like a pussy," I chuckled.

Steve turned to me and smiled, "What's your name again?"

"Karter."

"I like those tats, Karter. Like your old man too, he's a good dude."

"He's the best," I said.

"Let's go inside. Like any of the new bikes?" he asked as he pulled the door open.

I shrugged, "I don't know. I like that new Softail Slim, but I'm a starving artist. I can't afford a new bike. I just sold forty grand worth of art, but I have to manage my money. Hell, I might not sell anything else for six months."

"Don't cost anything to look, does it?" he asked.

"Nope," I responded as I walked through the door.

A new flat black Softail Slim sat in the middle of the showroom. As we approached it, Steve looked toward the bike and nodded, "Get on. It sits real low. Probably wouldn't even have to lower it."

I hopped on the bike and grabbed the bars. My feet sat flat on the floor and my knees were actually bent. Shocked, as I had to lower my Softail three inches to get it where I could safely ride it, I grinned at the stance of the bike. It fit me perfectly.

"How much?" I asked.

"$17,500 the way it sits. We'd give a little break off that," he said.

I kicked up the kickstand and felt the bike's weight against my legs. It was similar to mine, but almost twenty-five years newer and with a more comfortable seat. The thought of having a new bike was something that always appealed to me. I had no hang-ups with my bike, and felt no real reason to keep it other than I had almost no money invested in it. That, and the fact I couldn't afford to replace it. As I heard the unmistakable rumble of the Street Glide outside the front door, I tilted my head toward the entrance. Jak removed his helmet as he walked through the door.

"What'd you think of her, Jak?" Steve asked.

"Loved it," Jak smiled.

He looked truly happy. It was almost as if he finally found the escape he had needed all along. I realized there was a tremendous amount of burden carried by military war veterans, but Jak never talked about the war. As I wondered how he dealt with the emotion from all of the missions he'd been on, I considered the freedom he may have felt while riding the bike. Riding, for me, was an experience and an escape I could get nowhere else on this earth. As he slowly meandered through the showroom, he seemed to have a little more attitude to his walk.

In his boots, jeans, and tee shirt, he looked like a biker.

"Well?" I asked, trying not to sound too excited.

"Well what? Well, you look gorgeous on that new bike, honey," he smiled as he bent down to my height and kissed me.

"Do you like it?" he asked.

"Love it," I grinned.

"Would you ever trade in the other one?" he asked.

"Oh fuck yeah, if I could afford it. Truthfully, I hate that fucking Evo," I complained.

"How much for both of 'em?" Jak asked.

Oh my God. Don't fuck with me, Jak.

"Well, $27,500 for the 'Glide, and $17,500 for the Slim. That's $45,000. I'd say we could probably go $40,000 for them both," Steve responded.

"She's got a 1991 Softail in above average shape for the age. It needs a battery cable," Jak paused and looked toward me.

I smiled and pulled the battery cable from my rear pocket and held it in the air. If we ended up with two new bikes, there would be nowhere we couldn't go. Hell, if Jak wanted, we could ride to the coast. The thought of getting rid of my shitty old Harley became exciting as Steve waited for Jak to finish speaking.

"How about $35,000 and the old Softail?" Jak asked.

Holy shit. Jak's serious.

"Make it $36,500?" Steve asked.

"No," Jak responded.

Fuck, I'll toss in the fifteen hundred.

"I'll go $36,000," Jak said.

"You got a deal. Now what about her old bike?" Steve asked.

"I'll deliver it this afternoon," Jak responded.

"Sounds good, let's write it up," Steve said.

"Jak? You're serious?" I asked.

It all happened so fast. I'd never had anyone buy me anything, let alone something as expensive as a new bike. It was difficult for me to comprehend. Completely overwhelmed with emotion and excitement for Jak and me to be able to ride together, I waited for him to respond.

"Push it to the door, honey. Let's go get your bike and bring it back here, then we can spend the rest of the day riding," he grinned.

As I thought of loading the bike into the truck, I remembered the day Jak and I met, and how he lifted the back of the bike into the truck with ease.

And. I. Got. Wet.

As he began to walk toward Steve's office, I whistled. Jak turned around. I kicked the kickstand down and stood from the bike. I looked down at the waist of my jeans.

"Stick your hand in here," I laughed as I pulled the waist of my jeans away from my stomach.

"Let me get this signed and over with," he said as he tilted his head toward the office.

"Pussy," I whispered.

Fuck, I said that out loud.

Before I had a chance to make a run for it, Jak had me pinned to the floor, and his hand in my pants.

KARTER

Yeah, I think Jak will do just fine as a biker.

KARTER

I used to sit at home and worry Jak would simply forget about me one day. Having Jak be a part of my life made such improvements to me and my manner of living, I was afraid it would certainly come to an end. I had never truly enjoyed living until I met Jak. With him in my life, I viewed the world before me through different eyes, and not my colored contact lenses.

Life with Jak was not too good to be true, because it *was* true. It was real. And it was mine. And I, of all people, believed I deserved what I was being served as a repeated meal by the hand of no other than God. I had never really believed in God until after I met Jak. And now, I don't know how anyone could convince me God did not exist. Who could witness something as magical as the love Jak and I felt for one another, and believe it merely *happened*? Everything falling into place in the manner it had was far too complex to be anything but a plan by a being greater than man. I cleared my throat, set my coffee cup beside the newspaper, and closed my eyes.

God,

You keep Jak healthy, and I'll keep him happy. I can promise you that. And I don't make a promise if I don't intend to die keeping it. And you can take that to the fucking bank.

Shit.

KARTER

I probably shouldn't have cussed, huh? My bad. Rewind. Okay, keep him healthy, and I'll keep him happy. Pound it. Thanks for everything. Show me the way. Keep us safe out on the road. Shiny side up and all.

That's all I got.

Karter out.

I opened my eyes and began sorting through the piles of mail which had collected for almost the entire time I had known Jak. He had immediately consumed my entire life, and although it was in a good way, it was also a bit overwhelming looking at it from an outsider's point of view. As I flipped through the envelopes, one thing became immediately apparent.

The Sedgwick County Courthouse wanted to get ahold of me.

Desperately.

No less than six letters from the Sedgwick County Courthouse were amongst the mail I had inventoried. Frustrated, and assuming I had a warrant for my arrest, I grabbed my knife and cut the envelope open. I pulled the one page letter from the envelope and read it.

Mrs. Wilson,

Pursuant to case number SG-2436-17A, please provide proof of ongoing aftercare. If such proof isn't provided by August 28th, 2014, actions will be taken by the court.

Be reminded breach of the agreement set forth in the above referenced case may include fines, imprisonment, or both.

Circumstances of the case and of the agreement are available from the Clerk of the Court by providing the case number.

Respectfully,

The Prosecutor's Office

I tossed the letter on the counter.

Fuck.

I opened one of the other envelopes. The exact same letter with a different date was inside. I opened another. The same thing. Frustrated, I sat and stared at the newspaper I had just finished reading. I had been required by the court to attend no less than three Alcoholics Anonymous meetings as aftercare to my treatment. If not, I could be determined mentally incompetent by the court, and placed in an institution or in jail.

I shook my head, wrapped my hands around my coffee cup and thought of what my options were. I looked down at my cup and closed my eyes.

God,

Seriously?

I opened my eyes and shook my head. I glanced at the pile of mail and closed my eyes softly to close my prayer.

Karter out.

The August date had long since passed. Without a doubt in a short period of time, if not already, a warrant for my arrest would be issued. Frustrated, I picked up the phone and called the Prosecutor's Office. After three different people and twenty minutes of begging, I had authorization to attend three meetings in three weeks.

Thank God.

No pun intended.

A call to the treatment center revealed what I already knew. There were daily morning and afternoon meetings, seven days a week, 365 days a year. *Praise the Lord and pass the wicker basket.* I decided to send Jak a text and tell him the truth. He understood the importance of what I had to do, and we decided to meet for a late lunch afterward. After a quick shower and a wet ponytail I was on the elevator.

KARTER

I got off the elevator and looked at my new bike. It was a relief to have the old one long gone. It reminded me of my mother each time I thought about it. It was really the last thing that tied us together, and being rid of it would truly allow me to live a life free of any thoughts or attachments to her. I pulled my helmet on and fired up the bike. The rumble from the 1690 cc motor was totally different than the 1340. This bike was just like me.

Bad ass.

The ride through mid-morning traffic was without incident, and within fifteen minutes I was at the treatment center. After exchanging niceties with the counselor, I flopped down at the almost empty table, set my helmet on the floor, and looked around the room.

Three, including me.

I looked at my watch. It would be fifteen more minutes before the fun began. I rolled my eyes, looked up at the ceiling, and began counting the ceiling tiles. Generally, simple math would satisfy me when computing the size of a room. Considering my level of interest in being there, I decided I would count them individually to waste a little more time. When I reached 107, a familiar voice caught my attention.

"Nice to see you back, Karter."

I looked down from the ceiling.

Bill the bullshitter.

"Mornin' Bill," I sighed.

I leaned back in the chair and looked up at the ceiling.

Where was I?

Fuck, now I have to start over.

I saw the outline of Bill's body as he got a cup of coffee and sat in the same seat he was sitting in the day we met for the first time. I considered the fact he was at my very first meeting, he didn't attend any of the other meetings during my treatment, and now he had returned for my random assed unscheduled meeting. I began to wonder if he was following me. Not in a necessarily paranoid manner, but in a *what the fuck is the deal with this dude* manner. I stopped counting ceiling tiles at tile number 143, and shifted my gaze to Bill.

"So, *Bill*. Did you ever remember the name of the nineteen year old boy you slaughtered?"

He looked up from his cup of coffee and across the table. His eyes were filled with sorrow. *Real sorrow*. He nodded his head slowly and his lips began quiver as he started to speak.

"As a matter of fact, I did. It's been a tough week for me. It's why I'm here. I didn't rightly want to end up drunk again, so I decided it'd be better to come here and talk about it," he said softly.

I stared at him and began to feel sorry for him. But, without a name, it was still bullshit.

"What was his name?" I asked.

With a shaking hand, he lifted the coffee cup to his mouth and spoke over the top of the cup, "Well, I can't remember the last name, but I'm pretty sure I got the first. It was an odd one, just took some thinking to remember it."

Still bullshit, dude.

"And?" I asked, beginning to feel annoyed.

"Anderson. His first name was Anderson."

An immediate pain developed in my chest. My eyes welled with tears. I didn't immediately understand what was happening, but after a moment, I came to the realization Jak's father's name was Anderson.

In my very first meeting, Bill said he had the wreck on June 6th,

1976.

Jak was born in 1976.

In January.

I pushed myself from the table and stood. My eyes were swollen and full of tears. I stared at Bill. Without speaking or remembering to grab my helmet, I stumbled to my bike, fired it up, and twisted the throttle as far as it would go.

And the wind against my face dried the many tears of pain from what I was afraid to be the truth.

JAK

"So I've never asked, but lately I've started to wonder. Respectfully, I'd like to ask a personal question. Permission?" I chuckled.

"You ain't in the military anymore, boy. You ain't got to be askin' me permission to speak. Step away from the doorway so *the man* don't see ya," Oscar grinned as he waved his hand to the side.

I stepped into the shop and away from the door.

"Go on and speak your mind. What ya got?" Oscar said as he leaned against the golf cart and pulled a cigar from his pocket.

"Well, I was wondering. Is your wife still alive? Are you still married?" I asked.

"Well, thems two separate questions. She's gone, Jak. She died four years past. She died by the hand of a man who had one too many drinks on the eve of the new year. Makes that day a doozie for me. But the other question?" he paused and lit the cigar.

"Yessir. I's still married to her. Always will be. That's when you know it's true. When you stay married long after they's gone," he nodded as he pulled the cigar from his lips.

"I'm sorry," I sighed.

I had asked for other reasons, but knowing a little more about Oscar pleased me. He was a fine man, and brought a little more joy into what had become a wonderful life for me. Sharing time with people like him allowed me to understand the value of war. Good people fighting against the belief of evil for what they believed to be good. War was and will always remain terrible, but seeing the good in the world through the people in it provided me hope the fighting wasn't all for not.

"The reason I asked," I paused and walked toward the golf cart.

I opened my arms and smiled, "Thanksgiving is coming up. I was thinking if you had nowhere to go for the holiday, you could spend it with us. My mother, Karter and me."

"Thanksgivin' dinner. Whooooeeeee. Been a spell since I had me one a those. A real one. White folk eat turkey?" he asked.

"Yes, we eat turkey," I laughed.

He puffed on his cigar and widened his eyes comically, "You eat yams?"

"Yes sir."

He raised one eyebrow and stood erect, "Stuffin'?"

I nodded my head and laughed, "Yes, we eat stuffing."

"Hmmm. Well, if there's to be a certain pie at this gatherin', you might count this ole black man in. I likes me some peee-can pie. Any a you know how to make a good peee-can pie? You gots to make 'em with the Caro syrup, or you fuck 'em all up, ya see," he lowered his cigar, raised his chin slightly, and looked into my eyes.

"It's the only way my mother makes them. As much as I hate to admit it, this will be my first Thanksgiving at home in twenty-one years. Karter and I would love to have ya," I smiled.

"You mom let nigga's in the house?" he asked dryly.

I slumped my shoulders and shook my head in disbelief, "Well, I'll explain a little about my mother to you. If you use *that* word in her home, she'll escort you to the door. Everyone in my mother's home is equal. Everyone. If she hears that particular word fall from your lips, she'd politely ask you to leave. I feel the same way. So to answer your question, no. She doesn't let them in her home; because to her, and to me, they don't exist."

"I was kiddin' about bein' a nigga. Well, kinda. People have strange beliefs. Some of 'em, anyhow. I like you an' Miss Karter fo' sho'. You's good people. And I thank ya for askin'. If you's serious I'd sho' like to attend," he nodded.

"Well, consider it a date. My mother's expecting you. I told her about you some time ago, and she asked the other day. I said I'd ask."

"Miss Karter got a family?" he asked.

I shook my head, "I thought I told you. No, she doesn't. She's alone."

He shook his head and stared at the floor, "Maybe that's why I like her so much. I had me a little boy, Albert. We just called him Al. He died at fifty years. Same way as his momma. He was back east. Lived in Boston. Makes me kind a sick, so I don't drink me any of the devil's juice."

"I don't either, and you won't find any in my mother's home. I'm sorry about both your losses, Oscar," I said as I patted him on the shoulder.

"They's in a mighty fine place now, Jak. You God fearin' people?" he asked as he looked up.

I nodded my head sharply.

"Well, that's good. I'll say the prayer," he smiled.

"Sounds perfect. Well, I better get. I've got to meet her for lunch," I said as I rubbed my palms together.

He extended his hand and smiled. As I took his hand in mine and shook it, I tried to remember if we'd shaken hands before. As he released my hand, he grinned.

"I'll be seein' ya, Jak."

I smiled and walked to the door. As I passed the threshold, I tilted my head rearward.

"Not if I see you first."

KARTER

I'd used the microfiche machine at the library many times. I had tried to find out about my father when I was young by reading old newspapers on it in the library. Potwin, Kansas has no newspaper, and the news in Potwin wasn't of much interest to the people in Wichita, so there was nothing for me to find out about my mother or really anything regarding the small town I was from.

As I frantically searched though the film, I came across the June 6th newspaper and found nothing. It was a Sunday. As I moved to the film to the next day, the front page of the Local/State section stopped me from looking any further. A photo of the scene of the accident sent chills down my spine.

Two police officers stood beside a truck. The photo was of the old Kellogg Avenue. One officer stood in front of the truck and one beside it. The caption above the photo read *Drunken Driver Drags Man to His Death*. It wasn't the caption that caught my attention, it was the truck in the photo.

It was Jak's truck.

Holy mother of all things sacred.

Jak was still driving his father's truck. He had told me he used to drive the same truck in high school. Although he never spoke of his father, I knew he had died when Jak was young. His mother described how much she loved him, and Jak explained how he grew up without a father, but I never knew what happened for sure. And Jak never offered. Now I knew.

Bill killed Jak's father.

I sat at the machine and cried. I cried for Jak, for his mother, and for Bill. The thought of something happening so quickly, and how it could change the lives of so many people became very heavy in my chest. I sat and stared at the article on the screen blankly, not even caring to read any further.

As I wiped the tears from my eyes, I realized although I had solved a mystery of sorts about Jak's childhood, his past, and the death of his father, I could never share my findings with Jak. Keeping a secret from him wasn't something I really wanted to do, and even lying about my mother made me extremely uncomfortable. After much consideration and thought, I decided some things need to be kept secret to prevent further harm to those the secrets are kept from. When Jak was ready to tell me, he would. If he didn't, I'd take this knowledge with me to my grave.

Without removing the film from the machine, I stood and wiped my eyes. I left the light switch turned on and the article about Jak's father's death on the screen of the monitor. As I walked away, I did so with hope. Hope someone else would read the article and gain from it. If one drunken person took a taxi home instead of driving as a result of reading the article, the world would be a better place.

A much better place.

JAK

I sat across the table from the most beautiful woman in the world. As she picked her teeth with blade of her knife, I further realized just how extraordinary she truly was. If she were anything but one of a kind, she surely wouldn't fill all of what was broken within me with such precision. Karter was placed on this earth to make me whole. I further believed I provided her with the same satisfaction. As I admired her eye color choice for the day, she looked at the tip of her knife with disgust. A small piece of what appeared to be chicken hung from the blade. After wiping it on her jeans, she leaned into the center of the table.

"You ride like a pussy," Karter whispered.

I heard her clearly, but responded as if I had not.

"Say again?"

"*Say again*," she repeated in a mocking tone.

"I crossed my arms and tilted my chin upward, "What did you say."

"I said you ride like a pussy. And you still have a long fucking ways to go to be a biker, new beard or not. Oh, and your ears are getting weak, old man," she half shouted.

It seemed as if the entire rear portion of the restaurant turned around to see what the commotion was about. I lowered my chin and wrinkled my nose, "Old?"

I raised my hand to my chin and rubbed the four days growth of

KARTER

what was to be a new beard, "Pussy?"

"I knew you heard me," she said as she pushed her plate to the side and burped.

"Through these old ears?" I shrugged.

"Mmmmhhhhm," she mumbled.

"You're pushing your luck," I assured her.

"Oh really? What are you going to do? Punish me? By fucking me? Please Jak, please. I hate fucking you. Don't fuck me Jak. Please no. Not the sex. Anything but the sex," she said in a high pitched voice.

"That's it," I said as I slapped the table.

"You want me to bend over?" she asked.

I smiled at the thought of it. Karter was by all means the best thing to ever happen to me. She allowed me to understand just how simple living life could be - with the right person. I hadn't even attempted to imagine a life without her for some time; only what our future could and would bring us. Karter had taken me from wallowing in the guilt associated with war and breathed life into my lungs. I yearned for the arrival of June and our ability to officially be man and wife.

"As a matter of fact, I do. Get your ass in the bathroom. I'll be right behind you," I stood from my chair and removed my wallet.

"Seriously? The bathroom?" she squeaked as she pointed her finger over her shoulder and to the rear of the restaurant.

I cleared my throat and pointed to the bathroom, "Now, Karter. Go!"

She lowered her head, stood, and walked toward the bathroom. I dropped a fifty dollar bill on the table and covered it with my glass. I looked up and watched as Karter walked toward the hallway which led to the bathroom. As she walked with her shoulders slumped, I felt bad for acting stern. Surely she realized I was joking. As she entered the hallway, and was away from the view of the restaurant, she turned to face me and removed her shirt and bra. Now twirling them above her head, she took off in a dead run to the bathroom.

I shook my head and walked toward the bathroom. As I knocked on the door, she answered from the other side.

"Who is it?"

"Let me in," I said softly.

"Sorry, it's occupied."

I scanned the empty hallway. I beat my hand against the door sharply, "Open the door."

"Sorry, it's occupied," she said in an elevated tone.

I beat against the door with my clenched fist, "Karter, open the damned door."

She opened the door. Naked, except for her sneakers, she stood on the other side of the door.

"Oh, I thought you were someone else. Well, hurry up before someone sees me," she said as she waved her hand toward the large bathroom.

I stepped inside the door and locked it behind me. Her clothes were neatly folded on the sink. I reached toward the towel dispenser and smacked it sharply with the back of my fist. The hinged cover immediately fell open. I removed the towels, looked at Karter, and dropped them into the toilet.

"What the fuck was that about?" she whispered.

I flushed the toilet three times. Finally, the towels disappeared into the swirling water.

"Get on your knees," I demanded.

She smiled and lowered herself to her knees, "Oh, you going to face

KARTER

fuck me? Utter torture."

She closed her eyes and opened her mouth. Seeing her naked with her sneakers on was a huge turn on. I unzipped my jeans and pushed them to mid-thigh. As I positioned my cock onto her lips, she eagerly began to lick the shaft and suck the tip.

As she slurped and sucked, I pushed her to the wall between the sink and the trash receptacle. She opened her eyes and looked upward. As she watched the expression on my face, I began to push myself in and out of her throat forcefully. As my cock disappeared into her mouth I moaned loudly.

After several seconds of face-fucking as Karter described it, I was far too excited to continue. I wasn't done toying with her yet, and needed to change to something different to keep from reaching climax too quickly.

"Get up," I demanded as I pulled my saliva covered cock from her mouth.

She wiped her mouth with the back of her hand as she stood, "Oh, do you want this pussy?"

I looked around the bathroom. I had very few options, "Bend over the sink."

"Yes sir," she saluted as she spoke.

As she bent over the sink, she arched her back and raised her ass into the air. I looked down at the floor. She was on her tip-toes. Without a doubt, I wouldn't last long in this position. I waddled to the sink and gripped her waist in my hands. As I released her right side, I guided the head of my cock past her pussy lips and stood still. As I slapped her on the ass, I thrust myself deep into her in one forceful motion.

She grunted and buried her face in her folded clothes.

"Jesus, Jak. Thanks for the warning," she moaned.

I pounded away without reservation. As I eagerly watched myself disappear into her wet swollen mound repeatedly, she gripped the edge of the sink in her hands.

"Fuck me Jak," she grunted over her shoulder.

I worked my hips back and forth forcefully. As my upper thighs slapped against her ass, the sound of flesh on flesh echoed throughout the room. I released her waist and grabbed her hair. After collecting her hair in my hand, I pulled it rearward, arching her back even more. The angle of her body combined with my deep savage strokes was more than I was prepared for. After a half dozen aggressive thrusts, she began to groan.

"Harder…Jak…fuck me harder."

I pounded away as I looked down between the cheeks of her ass. My cock magically disappeared into her wet pussy with each thrust. I pulled her hair firmly as I forced myself into her. I felt myself beginning to swell. Within a few seconds, this would be over.

As I felt her begin to climax, I pulled my cock from inside her.

"On your knees," I demanded.

After a split-second hesitation, she turned and dropped to her knees.

"Fuck yes, cum in my mouth. I want to taste you," she said as she opened her mouth.

I stroked my swollen cock until I felt the pressure building. As I lowered the tip to her mouth, I felt myself begin to explode. As I began to spurt cum into her mouth, I moved the tip of my cock and sprayed her face with cum. The excitement of being in the bathroom, the eagerness of Karter to fuck in public, and the fact I had not reached climax in four days was apparent by the amount of cum covering her face. The last spurt landed directly in her falsely colored blue eye.

KARTER

As she looked up at me in a face of somewhat disgust, I gazed down and smiled.

"Jesus, what the fuck. Are you a porn star? You fucking covered me in that shit," she gasped.

I turned and shuffled to the toilet and removed the roll of toilet paper and flushed the toilet repeatedly until it disappeared. I turned to face her. Cum dripped from her chin onto her breasts as she attempted to wipe it from her eyes. I pulled my jeans from my thighs to my waist and stuffed my flaccid cock into them. As I buckled my belt, she turned toward me, still covered in cum with her eyes closed.

She held her hands in the air with squinted eyes, "Will you hand me something to clean this shit off?"

I reached for the door handle and smiled, knowing there was nothing but her clothes to wipe off with.

"You'll figure something out. My *old* eyes can't see too well."

I opened the door to the bathroom and walked to my bike.

And I felt more like a biker with each and every step.

KARTER

I finished reading the article on the front page of the Local/State section. Another driver killed due to alcohol consumption. Each and every one is disappointing in a different way. I stared at the page and wondered how many would truly be prevented if people simply either didn't drink or drank more responsibly.

I don't know that any one death is more important or holds any more value than another in the eyes of God, but this particular death, to me, provided an odd feeling of comfort. I sighed and turned the page to the obituaries.

As I scanned the obituaries, Jak walked toward the kitchen. Before I could get up, he was behind me, hugging me from behind. As he embraced me and kissed along my neck, he looked over my shoulder and down at the newspaper. He found it half morbid I read the obituaries every day, and had expressed it often. Some days, he asked if there was anyone important or interesting who had died. As I relaxed into his strong arms, his finger scanned the page of the paper. If I didn't know better, I would have sworn it stopped for a split second beside one of the names. I sighed and looked down.

His hand was gone.

Having already seen the article on the preceding page, I didn't need to read any more. I focused on the name.

KARTER

Shelley Peterson, 39, Potwin Kansas

He stood up, cleared his throat, and walked to the window. He stood shirtless and stared through the glass and up toward the sky for a long moment. I poured a cup of coffee and walked his direction. A new abstract painting of the open road was half complete on the easel. I hoped Jak would let me put in his apartment when I was finished. I placed the coffee on the desk in front of the window and lowered myself onto the stool. As I waited for Jak to drink his coffee, I sat and stared out the window and into the blue sky. As he continued to peer out the window, he cleared his throat.

"Anyone interesting pass away today?" he asked.

I shook my head and slid the coffee cup toward him, "Nope."

I stood from the stool and stepped his direction. Jak had been staying overnight more and more recently. We had both reached a point where it was difficult to sleep alone. When we were finally married and able to be together every night, my life would truly be complete.

He had trimmed his beard into a goatee of sorts, without the mustache. Although Jak was without a doubt the *man*, he wasn't *the man*. The mustache had to go. With his new haircut and a late summer tan from riding, Jak was perfectly gorgeous. As he reached out to hug me, I smiled and rested my head against his shoulder. Today we were going on a poker run. One of the stops was the bar in Potwin. Although I had been worried about going back to my home town, now I felt as if I could do so without much concern.

I decided if we encountered someone who knew me, I would deal with it at the time. I was done hiding from the truth. In some respects, I hoped someone *would* see me. I'd simply tell Jak the truth. Now, more than ever, I felt my past didn't matter so much. We all have a past. What we are willing to do and who we are willing to be from this day forward is truly what matters.

As Jak held me in his arms, I exhaled and slowly lifted my feet from the floor. As he felt my weight against his arms, he lifted me and let my legs dangle from the floor. As he held me tightly to his naked chest, he kissed me softly. Feeling as if I was truly in heaven, I closed my eyes and said a small prayer.

God,

I know they say you work in mysterious ways, so it comes as no surprise I can't often understand this crazy world we live in. Thanks for Jak, and for everything else you have graced me with.

Keep us safe today, and watch over everyone else we ride with. I know it's tough for you to understand, but I didn't really care one way or another about her. I imagine you'll have to sort her out and send her somewhere, so see if there's a place in heaven for her. She probably belongs in hell, but even though she was an evil woman, I'm sure she had her reasons. I won't make the funeral, but you know why.

I never cared much for her.

I suppose it's tough for you to understand, but it's my choice. I choose to love those who love me in return.

And I know that's why you gave me Jak.

Pound it.

Karter out.

EPILOGUE

I looked toward the doors as the music played. As they opened, she emerged into the aisle. It was the first time I had seen her in the wedding dress. She redefined beauty, just as Oscar had said.

As they walked the aisle, my breathing became labored. I knew if I were required to speak now, I'd be incapable. Overcome with emotion and joy, I simply wanted to watch my bride walk down the aisle.

I looked into the front row. My mother sat and softly cried. She hadn't attended my first wedding, and I was grateful. Seeing her joy now was worth a lifetime of waiting. She raised her handkerchief to her mouth as they stopped at the bottom of the aisle, not further than fifteen feet from where I stood.

"On this day, the 6th of June, before our Lord Christ, who gives this woman to be married to this man?" the preacher asked.

"I do, sir. Oscar Brown, sir," Oscar exclaimed with authority.

Oscar wore a black tuxedo with a tailed jacket. The tail from the jacket almost reached the floor. He looked magnificent. Although he had initially requested he be able to wear his Marine uniform, he decided against it when he learned I wanted no ties to the military in my wedding. Our lives were both beginning from scratch so to speak.

Karter had chosen the date of the wedding. June 6th. I had something very precious taken from me on this date as a child. This had been a day

KARTER

I had spent a lifetime associating with loss. It would now forever remain a day to celebrate love and the union of two people deeply in love. My mother, as I, could not have been happier. Secretly, she wanted Karter to allow her to pick the day, and reserved this day in her mind as hopeful.

The fact Karter chose it on her own caused my mother and I both to believe there was involvement from God above.

As the preacher spoke, I looked at Karter adoringly.

"Dearly beloved, we are gathered together here in the house of the Lord, and in the face of this company, to join together this man and this woman in holy matrimony, which is commended to be honorable among all men reverently, discreetly, advisedly and solemnly. Into this holy estate these two persons present now come to be joined. If any person can show just cause why they may not be joined together, let them speak now or forever hold their peace," he paused and exchanged glances between us.

"Marriage is the union of husband and wife in heart, body and mind. It is intended for their mutual joy, and for the help and comfort given on another in prosperity and adversity. But more importantly, it is a means through which a stable and loving environment may be attained. Through marriage, Jak Kennedy and Karter Wilson make a commitment together to face their disappointments – embrace their dreams – realize their hopes – and accept each other's failures. Jak and Karter will promise one another to aspire to these ideals throughout their lives together – through mutual understanding, openness, and sensitivity to each other."

"We are here today before God; because marriage is one of his most sacred wishes. We gather to witness the joining in marriage of Jak and Karter. This occasion marks the celebration of love and commitment with which this man and this woman begin their life together. And now, through me, he joins you together in one of the holiest bonds."

He smiled and lifted his bible to his chest. This was the part we both decided we liked the most.

"This is a beginning and a continuation of Jak and Karter's growth as individuals. With mutual care, respect, responsibility and knowledge comes the affirmation of each one's own life happiness, growth and freedom. With respect for individual boundaries comes the freedom to love unconditionally. This relationship stands for love, loyalty, honesty and trust, but most of all for their friendship. These two fortunate souls have never known friendship; only the deepest of love, from the first day they met and her feet were lifted from the floor," he grinned and nodded his head.

I smiled at Karter. God, I loved her. Only a few more minutes, and I could call her my wife.

"Do you, Jak, Take Karter to be your constant friend, faithful partner, and love from this day forward? In the presence of God, your family and friends, I ask you to provide your solemn vow to be her faithful riding partner and loyal friend in sickness and in health, in good times and in bad, and in joy as well as in sorrow. What say you, Jak?"

"I do," I said proudly.

"Do you, Karter, Take Jak to be your constant friend, faithful partner, and love from this day forward? In the presence of God, your family and friends, I ask you to provide your solemn vow to be his faithful riding partner and loyal friend in sickness and in health, in good times and in bad, and in joy as well as in sorrow. What say you, Karter?"

"I do," she responded.

He nodded his head. Oscar and my mother carried the rings to the preacher.

KARTER

We placed our rings on each other's fingers.

"By the power vested in me, I now pronounce you husband and wife. After you lift Karter from the floor and her legs dangle, you may kiss the bride," he grinned.

For the first time, I lifted her into my arms and kissed Karter as my beautiful wife.

And her legs dangled six inches from the floor.

Made in the USA
Charleston, SC
31 May 2015